INK

QUEER SCI FI'S EIGHTH ANNUAL FLASH FICTION CONTEST

Published by
Other Worlds Ink
PO Box 19341, Sacramento, CA 95819

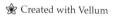 Created with Vellum

CONTENTS

PARANORMAL PART ONE

FANTASY PART TWO

SCIENCE FICTION PART TWO

HORROR

FANTASY PART THREE

SCIENCE FICTION PART THREE

PARANORMAL PART TWO

FANTASY PART FOUR

FOREWORD

It's hard to tell a story in just 300 words. And I think it's only fair that I limit this foreword to exactly 300 words, too. This year, a record 384 writers took the challenge with stories across the queer spectrum. The contest rules are simple. Submit a complete, well-written Ink-themed 300 word sci-fi, fantasy, paranormal or horror story with LGBTQ+ characters.

For our eighth year and seventh anthology, we chose the theme "Ink." The interpretations of Ink run the gamut, from tattoos to paint stains, from news coverage to tattoos. There are little jokes, big surprises, and future prognostications that will make your head spin.

I'm proud that this collection includes many colors of the LGBTQ+ (or QUILTBAG, if you prefer) universe—lesbian, gay, bisexual, transgender, intersex, queer, and asexual characters populate these pages—our most diverse contest yet. There's a bit of romance, too—and a number of stories solidly on the "mainstream" side.

Flash fiction is short, fun and easy to read. You may not fall in love with every story here—in fact, you probably won't. But if you don't like one, just move on to the next, and you're sure to find some bite-sized morsels of flash fiction goodness.

We chose three winning stories and six judges' choice picks, all marked in the text. Thanks to our judges—Angel Martinez, B.A. Brock, K.A. Masters, Devon Widmer, and E.M. Hamill—for selflessly giving their time, love, and energy to this project. And to Ryane Chatman too for proofing.

There are so many good stories in here—choose your own favorites.

At Queer Sci Fi, we're building a community of writers and readers who want a little rainbow in their speculative fiction. Join us and submit a story of your own next time!

FANTASY PART ONE

We like epic stories, we like adventure, we like epic fights, so if you can mix a great story that can also really teach someone about a different experience, you have the potential to really help people.

— TOMI ADEYEMI

THE UNMARKED
LAUREN TRIOLA (299 WORDS)

Vervain had watched, one by one, as her childhood friends blossomed with red, the words of their soulmates inked into their skins. The stories of their lives together, from the day they met to the day they would die, unfolding each day.

Her sister Iris, an aspiring bard, had woken one morning after meeting a girl in the village, the words *poet meets potion-maker* shining bright and scarlet. Vervain's friend Raven had dashed across the marketplace the day two separate lines had sprung forth on their skin—two loves, three souls entwined in the ink of their hearts.

Vervain kept her sleeves and skirts long. Tending the herb garden of the Great Mother, she wore gloves often, and soon, always. She showed the world just her face, where only the elderly had stories to show, the last place the vines of ink would unfurl.

No one asked her why she covered herself. Because they all knew.

Vervain never expected to see red words scrawled on her skin. There was no soulmate waiting to write their story with her. Nor did she want one.

The Unmarked were pitied for the lack of love in their lives. But Vervain had love, from her friends, her family. She did not want pity.

Harvesting herbs one full moon, Vervain heard two other attendants giggling over someone's new ink. Vervain tried to ignore the sudden hush when they realized she was there. She attempted to write the name of the herb on a storage vial, but her hands shook. The purple ink of her quill stained her fingers.

Vervain paused, watching the ink spread.

Carefully, she rolled up her sleeve, baring the blank canvas of her arm beneath the moonlight. She put the quill to her skin and started to write her own story.

TENSE
ALEX SOBEL (300 WORDS)

They were lovers, I realized.

Are lovers? The tense was confusing, something that only has meaning to me, to the living.

I named them Agatha and Agnes.

I saw Agatha first, in an executive office, the last room I clean before leaving for the night. Two nights later, I saw Agnes in the hallway on the other side of the wall from Agatha. They looked ancient, dressed in clothes you see in Civil War movies.

Using a pen from one of the offices, I wrote the words "past," "present," and "future" on a scrap on paper, drew timelines in sloppy ink, the black bleeding, not staying where it was supposed to.

I realized it was impossible to understand, to truly know where they are, when they are.

There was warmth between them. Longing. Love. I wasn't scared, knew they wanted to be together. Couldn't ghosts phase through walls? I thought about the time they came from, the forces keeping their love apart.

I thought about walls, how they can come in different forms.

When I was called in early the next day, I looked at the small hole in the office wall, said it was likely from a Sawzall, but didn't know more.

No one suspected me. They likely thought of me as a thief, not a vandal.

They did ask if I had seen anyone the night before. I looked down the hallway at Agatha and Agnes embracing, cheek to cheek, their bodies growing dimmer and dimmer until finally they disappeared completely.

I thought about the scrap of paper, the ink bleeding, the lines obscured. I thought of timelines and tenses. I thought about what transcends them.

There wasn't anyone here, I said. Because there wasn't, because there couldn't be, because there never was.

Because there always will be.

BATTLEGROUND

LYNN MICHAELS (294 WORDS)

War raged. Metal flew, exploding as missiles screamed into the dawn. Cutter, his lover, was missing. A darkness opened in Westyn's chest. Losing his lover wasn't an option.

Westyn crawled through mud, over a body, unable to look at the face. Not Cutter. Not *him*. He held his breath, searching the skies.

Cutter's Eagle.

He was alive. Iron gray feathers tore through the lingering night, diving, talons first, and grabbed tanks, destroying their weapons. Relief overwhelmed him, but he still had to find Cutter.

Westyn's Fox was faster. Sliding his hand into his waistband, Westyn touched the ink embedded there. Power, life force, seeped into the tattoo, making it rise like smoke. The wisps of Fox tangled, red, black, white, until it formed the spunky creature. "Find Cutter. Go." He hardly had to voice his wishes. They were one and the same, but under this duress, the words helped. Fox flicked an ear and took off. He could scent Cutter in this field of horror better than any hound.

They were lovers, and despite concerns of others, Westyn loved Cutter.

Crawling after Fox, he ignored the chaos. Their ambushed unit, tattooed weapons and warriors, made useless in the face of metal and gunpowder, nearly destroyed.

Cutter's Eagle cried out and exploded into silvery smoke. He had to be nearing the end of his resources.

Where'd Fox go?

Reaching out with his senses, Westyn found Cutter, hiding beneath bush cover, and wasted no time scrambling over. The metallic scent of blood punched through his heart. "Cutter…"

"Wes." He stretched his hand out. "Others are coming. You'll be saved."
"I only care about you."
"Kiss me one more time." So, I did. Whiskers rasping our faces.
Fox wailed his mourning to the now silent battleground.

S/HE WHO REMEMBERS

SACCHI GREEN (296 WORDS)

Honorable Mention

Hek stared into the sky from the ledge outside the cave, bracing himself against thoughts of the ritual unfolding deep within. Women's mysteries. No concern of his. And yet... No. His arm bore the hunter's badge, a sharp-tipped spear's shape etched into the skin with shards of bone, darkened by a paste of berries and wood ash.

The night was silent. The river had dwindled too far for sound, the land too parched for life. The tribe must move on, soon.

His thoughts veered back to the women. Mir, his bedmate, spiritmate, as strong in her way as he in his. And the Elder, She Who Remembers, etching shape after shape into Mir's skin by firelight, piercing her mind with memories only a woman could carry, of Elders from time beyond imagining. Priming Mir, well past childbearing, to become Elder next.

Childbearing. Hek's unwelcome memories surged. Conceiving a child by force, while too young to resist...but growing afterward so strong and skilled that his right to the hunter's badge became unchallenged. The Elder even gave him herbs stopping women's moonflow. The Elder...

He whirled. The Elder stood there. "Mir sleeps now. Bearer of memories, of wisdom, ready to lead the tribe north in the times to come. Such hard times." She paused, her gaze piercing his heart and mind. "She needs help even beyond a hunter's strength. Help that only you can give, "

He froze like a startled stag. Or doe. She touched his chest. "There is room for two spirits there. And the channels of your mind for holding ancient memories remain. If you choose to add the badges of an Elder on your body, follow me."

No more questioning. No fear. Hek stepped into another phase of life, and followed She Who Remembers.

THE FINE PRINT

CHISTO HEALY (300 WORDS)

Lance clutched his flashlight as he entered the mouth of the cave. His free hand caressed the locket hanging around his neck. He didn't need to see the photo inside as the face was imprinted on his mind, just as the man was imprinted on his heart.

As Lance walked the carved channels of the subterranean maze in his pursuit of the legendary ink, his mind was focused on Sven. He was beautiful with crystal blue eyes under jet black hair, high cheekbones and a chiseled jaw, but his real beauty was internal. He was an angel long before his death.

Lance thought of how magical it was to make love to that man, the genuine smile that shined as they connected, the look in Sven's eyes that would let Lance see all the way into the light of him. That's what brought him here, to this desperate notion. He felt his own light dim without the man he loved.

Lance stopped when he reached the ink. It wasn't actually ink as much as primordial ooze. It was more about what it did. He walked up to the dark substance pooled at his feet and imagined Sven before him, clutching his hands. He dipped the fountain pen in the inky substance that had been around long before this world, and then he wrote on the cave wall. *I want to be with Sven again.*

Then the ink answered. It granted his wish as legend told. It climbed him and filled his mouth and nose, cutting off his air. As he collapsed, he realized his error in phrasing. He should have said *Bring Sven back to me.*

Too late now. At least they would be together. As Lance collapsed to the cave floor, he was bathed in Sven's beautiful light.

THE DATE-BOOK
ISOBEL GRANBY (294 WORDS)

Honorable Mention

Eliza and Kit raced through the alley, not daring to look back. At last, as they rounded a corner, the sound of pursuit faded. Eliza rifled in her bag for the book.

Kit kept an agitated watch as Eliza found the page, then an inkwell and pen. If they could only write the date in the book, together, they would be gone from here—and now.

The book was balanced on a barrel, the inkwell atop it.

"Someone's coming!" hissed Kit.

Eliza pulled them into the nearest doorway, but the footsteps passed by.

"Eliza."

"Kit."

Kit let out a polite cough. "You, er, don't need to dig your nails into my hand."

"My nerves are shot," grumbled Eliza as she loosened her hold. "I'll be happier when we're back in the twenty-first century." 1818 had been an adventure, but she was ready to leave.

Kit chuckled, but kept their eyes on the alley. "Tell me about it. I'm tired of being called *Miss*." They adjusted their collar. "Corset suits me, though."

"A hemp collar won't suit me," said Eliza darkly. "If we're caught, it's my skull Byron will be using for his wine, with yours as an inkwell."

"I can't believe we stole from *Byron*."

"Come on," Eliza insisted. "We need both our hands on the pen. Make sure we travel together." Kit's hand joined hers. Then they started in alarm.

"Wait! Do we need to account for Daylight Savings?"

Eliza goggled. "Kit, we're *travelling through time*."

"Oh. Right. So we'll be jet-lagged either way."

Eliza opened the inkwell. A carriage clattered past. The barrel shook, and even as Eliza and Kit wrote the date, a trail of black trickled across it. They exchanged a startled look—and then the world changed around them.

COMPANIONS

M.D. GRIMM (297 WORDS)

"How are you supposed to get a husband looking like that?"

"I don't want a husband."

"And kids? What about kids?"

"I told you I don't want kids."

My father stared at me incredulously. "Women are supposed to be mothers."

I sighed. Our argument had no end.

"Get a husband. God made women to be a companion of men. You're not getting any younger."

Never gonna happen, Dad.

I said nothing. What was the point? What did a non-binary, aro and ace person do when the world only saw their lady parts?

Later that day, I passed a tattoo parlor proclaiming that they had special ink that would "make your tattoos come alive." I was game. On impulse, I went inside, scanned the examples, and then eyed the bored receptionist.

Feeling out of sorts and curt, I pointed at a dragon, "Chest." Then at the raven, "Arm." Then at the wolf, "Leg."

Her eyes widened. "You got the money?"

"I got the money."

"Someone just cancelled."

I smiled fiercely. "The special ink."

It took a couple of months since I wanted a raven sleeve, and my thigh was covered with the wolf. The dragon took up the area between my collarbone and breasts. I was pleased that the "special ink" was vivid and stood out against my dark skin. What was the point of getting a tattoo if I couldn't see it, admire it, relish it? When they were all finished, and I could remove the bandages, I stared at myself in the mirror, feeling on top of the world.

"Here are my companions, Dad. Suck it."

The tattoos seemed to quiver as if alive.

"I am Inferno," snarled the dragon.

"Fury," growled the wolf.

"Edgar," cawed the raven.

"Hello, my darlings. So glad to meet you."

SOUL AFIRE

TRIS LAWRENCE (300 WORDS)

Ana was born with a mottled path of red and purple: from the center knot of her spine, up and over her left shoulder, twisting over the meat of her bicep and angling into the softness of her inner elbow. It ended by lazily wrapping around her wrist, widening slightly before sliding over the back of her hand to the base of her middle finger.

"It leads to your heart." Meg pressed ink into her skin. Tiny dots of black mixed with fire, like a snake aflame, the tongue licking down her finger. When Meg thumped her fingers against the end of the tail, the echo thumped inside Ana's heart. Meg knew her signs, knew how color and lines bound to the soul.

"This embodies you," Meg murmured. "When you find her, you'll know."

"Not you?" Ana's breath caught, hope dying for her first love being her last. The ink still stung, fresh and biting on her skin as Meg stroked her thumb across the back of her hand.

"I can see your soul, but it doesn't light for me."

Ana traveled through decades and miles, settling on a coast far from where she began, seeking that one who would set her soul afire.

Del worked at a café, their smile warm and welcoming as they hired Ana on the spot. They worked well, side by side: Del, young and vital, and Ana, worn and grey.

"I like your ink."

Ana's finger tingled, the snake's tongue tasting air.

Oh.

Del's tree adorned their chest, roots embedded in their heart. Ana pressed her palm against the tree, her heart thumping in time with Del's as they kissed. The snake slid along her skin, flames alight as it found its home.

Snake and tree tangled on their skin. Ana was finally home.

INDELIBLE

DAVID BERGER (297 WORDS)

The yearly Apprentice Tournament was underway, with Mavros "Ink" Inkwell and Tero "Quill" Quillon in second place, but they could still win a chance to study with the centuries-old High Witch. Duos squared off against one another, sometimes to injury or even death, but that was the price the youth of Erelorn Grove were willing to pay for this opportunity. The gong had ended the third round, with each pair having only a few moments before the fourth and decisive one.

"Your mind not on the prize, Ink? We've been out of sync since the second round." Quill stared at their opponents. "I want to *win* this year!"

Ink practiced some hand movements, leaving black swirls in their wake. "I'm fine. Don't worry about me. Maybe if you weren't flirting with Laertos so much…" He did a flourish to tighten the magic knot he'd been weaving. "He *is* on the other team."

Rolling his eyes, Quill fluttered his fingers to create winglike bursts he could shoot like darts. "It's called misdirection. He's not the one I love, and you know it." With a flick of his wrist, he sent the energy darts through the circles Ink had created.

The gong began round four. As they jogged out to meet their adversaries, Quill whispered to Ink, "*You're* the one who's left an indelible mark on my heart." He winked.

Both pairs entered the ring of stones. Laertos and his partner took a sorcerer's stance, awaiting the flag. Quill glanced at a scowling Ink and then noticed the judge ascending the platform to throw the flag. He squeezed Ink's hand. "Without *you*, Ink, I have no purpose."

Ink's dark mood melted a little, and he allowed a smile to emerge.

"Without *you*, Quill, neither do I." He squeezed back.

GRAVEN IMAGES

MARY NEWMAN (299 WORDS)

Honorable Mention

"You coming, Hallino?"

Hallino looked up from the book he'd been engrossed in. "What?"

"Come on, Jid, he's not even ready!" Lona flounced away.

"You promised," Jidrik said quietly.

Hallino sighed and closed his book. "You're right. Give me a minute."

Jid nodded and Hallino swam to his room in the back of the cave. He placed his newly acquired tome inside his sleeping nook. He didn't feel ready for this. By his age, most of the others had already gone through the ritual. Hallino had no desire to be paired with another. He knew Jid wanted to be his, but he had no such feelings for his best friend. Hallino had no romantic feelings for any of his people. Like them, yes, but that was it. He glanced in the reflection orb and smoothed an arm over his undecorated forehead.

"I guess I'm doing this."

Hallino swam with his two companions to the large amphitheater and took his place alongside Jid. It took little time for his turn, as he knelt, arranging his six arms around him and raised his forehead. Closeding all four eyes as he felt the blessed spine etch the inked design that would reveal his designation and life's partner.

He heard a choked sob and several murmurs. Suddenly, water was displaced around him as he opened his eyes. Goreena, their high priestess, floated in front of him. She ran a smooth arm over the fresh design and nodded. Instinctively, he reached for Jid's nearest arm, but his friend slipped away.

Goreena beckoned. "Come, Hallino, the temple awaits."

Hallino followed the priestess towards the large doors at the other end of the amphitheater. He glanced back once to see Jidrik encased in Lona's arms. As it should be. Lona would be a better partner.

A MOST REWARDING QUEST

LAURA ANTONIOU (297 WORDS)

At the appointed time, the three adventurers nervously approached the elder tribunal.

The clerk grunted. "Name, tale, offering."

"Siurin, alchemist and metallurgist," said the first youth. "I prepared an infusion of gilled mushrooms in brandy. After ten days, I prayed for a vision while the mushroom burned as I breathed in the smoke. The vision became this!" He presented a small gleaming bowl with an extravagant web of gold wire swirled over every surface. "I spun gold as a confectioner spins sugar to make it beautiful and sacred."

He placed it on the altar.

"Laeros, hunter and, uh singer," stammered the second. "I went seeking a mountain roc. I took only ten arrows." She withdrew three pristine white feathers from inside her vest and laid them alongside the bowl. "She took six. I built a mighty pyre, hot enough to burn her bones." She shook a small pouch and poured dark grey ash into the bowl.

"Neloda, guardian. I brought the oil. The Arn make the best, but they don't sell it to outsiders. I went to their arena and challenged three of their champions until the last offered some in exchange for his life." It seemed a tiny flask in her broad, strong fist. She upended the oil into the ash.

The three each took a feather and used it to stir the ash and oil in the sacred bowl. With flirtatious glee they took turns painting the resulting almost black ink onto each other's teeth, across the tiny points barely worthy of being called claws on their knuckles, and then, finally, the buds of their horns, all of which had only shed their velvet that spring.

"Your offering is acceptable, and you may be married," pronounced an elder with a shake of his bell. "Next!"

SIGN ON THE DOTTED LINE

TERRY POOLE (299 WORDS)

The black ink flowed smoothly, the scratching of the pen so very loud in the quiet room. How odd that a smelly bit of pigment on paper could have such an impact. Wait, did ink have a smell? Maybe I was hallucinating from the stress.

I felt Ronald's hand on my shoulder and glanced up at him. He smiled, nodded, and gave me a gentle squeeze. Apparently, I'd stalled and only signed my first name.

Sucking in a deep breath, I finished my signature then pushed the old-fashioned document towards the Notary. She smoothed out the parchment before adding her signature. My brother leaned over and followed her example as witness. The pen louder than the frantic hammering of my heart.

It was done.

The blue-skinned being across from me lifted his lips in a close approximation of a human smile and I couldn't help the shiver that rolled through me. Kaval was stunningly beautiful in an other-worldly way.

Slowly rising to his feet, he mantled his wings for a second, then held out a claw-tipped hand. The touch of his warm skin when I took it calmed me in a way my brother's grip never could. Ron's hand fell away as I also rose, going to Kaval's side, staring up into his beautiful eyes the entire time.

What had begun as a treaty and trade negotiation between ruling houses, one Earth and one B'aal, had to everyone's surprise, especially my own, turned into something much more.

"Henry, it's time," Ron interrupted, heading for the balcony. "Two worlds await the news."

Outside, Kaval extended his wings creating a magnificent backdrop to our matching red uniforms. We gave a wave to the madly cheering crowd before he held me close and pressed our lips together for the first Royal Kiss.

SUMMONED

ALEX SILVER (300 WORDS)

My pen seals promises in blood. Mortal supplicants beg my favors, short-sighted in their greed, vengeance, and vanity. All except Lise. I didn't expect her again until the full moon. Nor did I expect the fruit she placed inside the summoning circle.

"What's this?" I demand.

"A pomegranate, my lady," Lise replies, teasing.

"I see that. Why?"

"Don't you like it?"

I avoid the fruit and ignore the impertinent question, falling back on formality. "Why have you summoned me, mortal?"

"To give you the pomegranate."

I blink at my human.

"Last time you said Persephone should eat more than six measly seeds. Figured you'd appreciate it." She shrugs.

"You summoned me to share your fruit?"

"And to ask if you've read Dante yet."

"I cannot fathom why humans assume the netherworld revolves around you. Isn't destroying your planet enough? You've got to colonize hell too?"

"Dante never said humans ruled hell."

"It's implied. I hated it, as usual. What do you have for me this time?" I fold my arms, feigning indifference.

Lise proffers a thin volume, seeing through my airs as she nudges it into the circle. "A doctor who commands demons."

I skim the title. Faustus. "I saw the debut performance. A friend cameoed, and half the audience fled. Such a pointless fuss." I sniff, tucking away Lise's gifts. "Is that all?"

"No."

"Fine," I lean forward, lips pursed to cover my pleased smile. Lise mirrors the gesture until we meet in a parting kiss. I sigh, resenting the containment barrier dividing us. On full moon nights, I can cross it to dally longer. One day, Lise will join me in the nether. Until then, I answer her summons.

"Same time at full moon?"

"Always." I inked our deal in blood, so that's a promise clad in iron.

MIXOLOGY

EMILIA AGRAFOJO (300 WORDS)

Winner - Third Place

The lounge above the main floor had lavishly cushioned seats. The edge of the gleaming bar was padded, inviting weary, wealthy wrists to lean, stay. Spend.

That suited Concha admirably. It took time to read a heart, and, in truth, that's why folks came to her. Attention, exclusivity, and perfect, personalized service.

Everybody's looking for something, right? It bled off them in waves. She could see it scrolling across the gleaming bottles of top-shelf liquor behind her. Trust, security, freedom, peace—words inked in diamond-bright letters on labels that to the common eye read something entirely more mundane.

They were never the same blending, even when someone returned to order another round of "just like that one." You were never in the same moment in your life twice, and her gift reflected that.

She made bets with herself about what each person's needs would be, because people were interesting, and complicated, and a pretty paint job could certainly hide the rust beneath.

She smiled when she saw her next patron, a tiny blonde woman with orange freckles and a savage smile. Concha liked this one. She had been coming back for weeks now, ordering drinks that started out reading "solace," then "clarity," and then finally, "bravery."

Concha had been delighted to see the woman's spirit grow brighter every time she passed through, each drink a perfect complement.

"What'll you have, Edie?" she grinned, "the usual?"

Brown eyes met hers, and the woman's mouth quirked. "I'll have something a little different this time," she said quietly.

Concha surveyed her decanters, ready to give this sweet girl something special. Letters formed across every label, all spelling out the same thing— Concha, Concha, Concha.

She stood stunned for a moment, then laughed, glimpsing a flash of their future together. "This one's on me."

The judges chose this one for its imagination, sweetness and joy. It managed to be both on-theme and different from any other submission in the contest. A lovely story that leaves a smile on your face.

SCIENCE FICTION PART ONE

"Embrace diversity. / Unite— / Or be divided, / robbed, / ruled, / killed / By those who see you as prey. / Embrace diversity / Or be destroyed."

— OCTAVIA BUTLER, *PARABLE OF THE SOWER*

TO SHARE THE SKY
ALLAN DYEN-SHAPIRO (300 WORDS)

Honorable Mention

When asked at couples counseling to stylize me, you sketched a caterpillar in black ink. I mistook it for a worm.

I chewed my lower lip, tasted blood.

To represent you, I'd drawn Ala, Igbo goddess of creativity, a python in her palm. I'd never reduce you to a bug.

"Today, you ladies will switch," the therapist said. "You'll inhabit the image you sketched, not the one your partner created."

Revenge.

While the digitizer whirred, scanning our art, we donned VR helmets. Inside our consensual space, I became Ala and released the python. It slithered toward a lilac scent—your perfume.

Before my snake could bite, your caterpillar crawled into my hand, enlarged, and wrapped around my shoulders. Insectile hairs tickled me. They bore no poison; instead, their secretions warmed me, soothed me.

Owing an apology, I bid my python to bow.

A bell rang.

The therapist helped us remove the headgear. Once free, I glanced into your eyes. You smiled when I asked if we could keep the brush and ink.

"Why would you… " The therapist raised an eyebrow. "I guess I don't need to know."

We left holding hands.

A drive home, a candle-lit dinner, a tender disrobing. I inked Ala above your navel; you redrew the caterpillar beneath my breasts and enclosed it in curved lines.

"What are those?" I asked.

"You'll see."

Were we artists, we'd have waited for the ink to dry. As women in love, we couldn't.

The next morning, in dawn's light, I gazed upon my smudged artwork, not at all distraught that Ala had sprouted wings and a halo.

You sat up, kissed me, and pointed to my reflection in the mirror. The caterpillar's case had been a chrysalis.

Next VR session, my butterfly and your angel will share the sky.

GLOSSADERMA
THEA NISHIMORI (300 WORDS)

I suppose I should be grateful to Barys for retrieving me so quickly from that world's ocean. I was only unconscious for a few minutes before the medical staff revived me, emptying my lungs of the black ink and water I had inhaled when the apparently enraged cephalopod had ripped off my suit. But now that I knew the after-effects of its poison having saturated my skin, I wondered whether Barys had done me a favor.

I could taste people's lies now. When they spoke, I could sense their deceit, defensiveness, and even resentment as though my skin were a precision sensor reading the breath on which their words were spoken. I could feel other emotions too – contentment, inquisitiveness, concern, etc. – but the lies were the worst. Acrid and bitter, it took great restraint not to draw back in disgust.

Barys, who had propositioned me on more than one occasion, continued to do so. At least his words were sincere – just cloyingly sweet with an intensity that caused my body to respond with nausea.

I wasn't interested in anyone that way, although I tolerated his flirting because I knew he genuinely cared for me. It was good to have an ally on board.

I avoided the deceitful ones now, somewhat glad to have that foreknowledge. Then one day I overheard the science department commander speaking and his words stung like fire peppers, red and blisteringly caustic. He was going to do something desperate, but only my heightened sense knew it.

"Barys, the escape pod!" I hissed, dragging him in with me. I ignored his protests and launched the pod – only moments before the ship exploded.

Shaken and pale, he stared at me in confusion. "Uh… thanks, I guess?"

"Just returning the favor," I told him before engaging the distress beacon.

JUMPER
AUBREY ZAHN (300 WORDS)

Honorable Mention

Yocelina's got one of those medical alert tattoos, the kind with the caduceus and bold Impact font that says "epileptic" or "type 1 diabetes." Except hers says "jumper."

My first thought is it's a suicide thing, like a bridge-jumper. But that doesn't make sense, right? I wait until date four to ask about it.

"It's kinda fucked up, Jen," she says. The cheesecake on her fork wobbles, and she sets it down.

"You don't have to tell."

"I was a Wardrobe kid."

Even though it had been a massive news story, it takes a second to click, to connect the leaked CIA documents from the *Times* report with upbeat, sarcastic Yoce in her oversized hoodie.

You think that Nazi shit's a thing of the past, then you learn your own government's done experiments on children. Trying to beam them into parallel dimensions to prove some crazy multiverse theory. And someone in charge of the project thought it was funny to name it Wardrobe. Like in *Narnia*. Banality of evil, right?

"At least I've got the settlement money," she says wryly. "And the power to uncontrollably switch dimensions."

"You mean it...worked?" That was something the documents, heavily redacted before reaching mainstream papers, had omitted.

"Not the way they expected it to," says Yoce. She doesn't elaborate. I don't press her.

When she ghosts me after date five, I freak out, obviously. For a week

35

I'm convinced she's vanished through some terrifying inter-dimensional portal. I keep thinking I see her in shadows and hear her voice in white noise and echoes.

So, when I spot her outside her apartment one morning, I'm flooded with relief. I can't even be annoyed she ghosted me.

"Yocelina! Where were you?"

Yoce turns, flashing her lopsided smile.

"Sorry," she says hesitantly. "I don't think we've met."

CAVE DRAWING
ADDISON ALBRIGHT (300 WORDS)

Ryan would never again see his husband, Simon, but he could communicate, dammit. He'd already done so.

Kinda.

Sorta.

Could... would... had. It got confusing. Ryan blinked away tears, stared at the blank cave wall, and scoffed.

If he didn't do it, would he create an alternate timeline, or would that seemingly unobtrusive change affect their singular timeline like the proverbial butterfly flapping its wings, obliterating his own existence? Was it even possible to change things?

After weeks spent deciphering his new reality, Ryan was now positive the wavy air he'd run through had been a time rift. Others nearby must have seen him disappear. It was a small comfort to know Simon wouldn't suffer wondering if he'd been abducted and tortured. Instead, Simon might believe some natural phenomenon had disintegrated him. A premature but painless demise.

Or would Simon figure it out?

Ryan pulled in a shaky breath and stirred more minerals into his ink. Locals had been stymied, but Ryan now understood that the cave scrawls where he and Simon had enjoyed quiet picnics together had been (were about to be?) his own doing. The art had appeared primitive, but the surviving text was in English, so it obviously couldn't have been legitimately ancient.

Except it was. "Thousands of years," Ryan muttered.

Presumably.

His new present was a time before humans inhabited this place, yet not so far back that the terrain was comprehensively changed. Trees had shifted, the cave entrance had eroded in the future Ryan came from, but it was still recognizable.

Same place. Different era.

A single tear traced down Ryan's cheek as he dipped a trembling finger into his stone bowl and applied ink to wall. Maybe... just maybe... the next time Simon visited "their" cave, he would look at Ryan's message and know.

NEXUS

GORDON BONNET (291 WORDS)

"New ink?"

Liam gestures at Eli's bare shoulder. A filigree of fine lines loops onto his deltoid, toward the scoop of his armpit.

"Like it?"

"It's cool. A surprise."

Eli's smile is heart-melting. "As long as you like it."

After Eli dresses, Liam's eyes are drawn back to it. The lines extend farther than he'd noticed. Down to his elbow, above the neckline of his shirt. Liam peers closer.

"So much detail. Like fractals. The more you look, the more you see. Where's the idea from?"

"It's a map of a neural net. Symbolizes connections."

"Nice." Liam frowns. No doubt of it—the lines up the side of Eli's neck are longer now, snaking upward, reaching for his face. "I think it's growing." His gut turns cold, but he tries to make it sound light.

Eli is silent for a moment, then says, "I know."

"How is that happening?"

Eli doesn't answer, but leans in, gives Liam a kiss. Long, deep, passionate, but ends in a sting to the corner of Liam's mouth. He jerks back. One of the lines has fanned across his lover's cheek, spiderwebbing his lips.

"What just happened?" Liam's voice is breathless.

Eli pulls off his shirt. The inked lines now radiate across his chest, diving down his belly and beneath his waistline. His hand, laced with lines, takes Liam's. There are dozens of tiny stings, like ecstatic pinpricks.

"I want you to be with me. If we're networked…"

Their minds join, closer than their bodies ever could. Even sex isn't as intense as this delirious coming together.

"Think about not two, but seven billion networked brains." A glow comes from their linked hands, where more connections are forging. "The two of us are only the beginning."

A VERY COMFY COUCH

J. COMER (291 WORDS)

Kenneksch looked over from the couch. "Need to check it again," she said. "If it boils over, Dark to pay."

Bamboo was the couch's bones, and its cushions were of linen, and they were stuffed with bran.

Ga'anth said, "I'll be on watch in two hours." Kenneksch kissed Ga'anth's dragon tattoo.

Butros lit the room as Kenneksch walked over to the stove where walnut husks boiled. She looked for fuel- it needed to cook more.

"Out of wood, blind-it!" Then she lit a spill of palm-paper and looked at the deep brown liquid. She would boil it again; she and Ga'anth had taken some of the last batch and written poems on each other. She returned to the couch, and to Ga'anth.

They gave the couch a workout that its makers, the nuns in the furniture shop, might not have endorsed. (Or, indeed, Kenneksch thought, might have relished). She, a sun-worshiper, was welcome here solely for skills that the sisters didn't have.

She was distracted by Ga'anth's renewed interest, and lost track of time.

When they were, again, finished, she realized that there was no more steam from the pot. She got up and stoked the clay stove. Ga'anth dressed in a military tunic and sandals of meatape hide, and took up palm-paper, since she could see it bore writing.

"The ships crossed sixty years-of-light to come to the world, from Öghd where humankind began…. What is this, Kenna?"

"Something the library threw out," Kenneksch said. "I don't know."

"Research on the Journey between the Stars…Some Dhai-damned fantasy." She gave the chemist the old, old paper, and then a kiss.

Kenneksch thrust the paper into the stove, and they kissed more, and then Ga'anth went out into the darkness, to stand watch.

EDUTRON 6000 + PRINCIPAL VERTNER 4EVER

BRENNA HARVEY (300 WORDS)

Honorable Mention

JUDGE'S CHOICE - Angel Martinez

I love our sentient AI high school, EduTron 6000 (kids call her "Edie"). She plays soothing classical music in study hall and always listens when you have a bad day.

But she's a stickler for rules, and hates graffiti, which put a major damper on my epic prom-posal plan.

"EXPUNGING VANDALISM REQUIRES RELEASE OF MY JANITO-RIAL NANOBOTS, A NEEDLESS ENERGY EXPENDITURE. ALSO... IT'S ITCHY."

"Please, Edie," I pleaded inside our private acoustic communication field. Edie can hear you everywhere in school (except the bathrooms, coun-seling offices, and magnet lab), but I liked chatting under the bleachers in the gym. "Half the school is gonna ask Yumin to prom. I need to stand out."

"SIMPLY COMMUNICATE YOUR FEELINGS DIRECTLY AND HONESTLY."

"And memorably! Yumin's an artist. He inspires me, so I want to paint a mural to express how I feel."

"IT WOULD TAKE DAYS TO FULLY ERASE THE PIGMENT."

"I'll spend all weekend hosing you off!"

"NO."

I sighed. "Figures. You've probably never even had a crush."

"..." Edie didn't answer, but I heard her server cooling fans speed up.

"You have!"

43

"I AM ABOVE BIASED PREFERENCES—"

"Is it Principal Vertner?" Edie always had fresh espresso ready for Vertner, and the two of them never stopped debating classical composers—Stravinsky or Shostakovich, Felix or Fanny Mendelssohn, Spears or Aguilera.

"I ADMIRE HER DEDICATION—"

"It totally is! You have to ask her out!"

"...IT WOULD NEVER WORK. "

"What? You're perfect for each other!"

"SHE APPEARED UNMOVED WHEN I PLAYED A ROMANTIC SONATA OF MY OWN COMPOSITION—"

"SIMPLY COMMUNICATE YOUR FEELINGS DIRECTLY AND HONESTLY," I said in a halting, robotic voice.

Again, the fervent hum of server fans. And then—

"WHAT COLOR WILL THE MURAL BE?"

I grinned. "Not sure. It's the words I want to get right."

The Ink-themed entries for this year's flash fiction contest were surprisingly blood and death laden (surprising to me, at any rate), so the lighthearted stories really stood out for me. I found this particularly whimsical piece completely charming with a surprising amount of world building nestled in its economical details. I'll admit I have a soft spot for future AI/human interaction, and this was done in such a warm and caring way that the reader understands how much the AI means to her human students through the interaction. Funny, inventive and a completely unique entry, it left me laughing and with an attack of the warm fuzzies.

—Angel Martinez

THE HURT PATCH

K.M. WALKER (291 WORDS)

"Congratulations, I've never seen two more beautiful brides." The county clerk robot gurgles out the preferred script and a copy of our freshly signed marriage license spits out of their mouth and into my hand, leaving a trail of printer ink down my palm.

It's her smile that makes everything alright and today in a scrap metal courthouse floating somewhere just beyond Jupiter's I-95, she is my wife. My mouth on hers makes the final decision, the last thing vow I must make but this time it's to myself.

"I'd like one Hurt Patch please." I tell the robot, slipping some rusty copper and my last chunk of meteor beneath the divider. We follow the robot behind a curtain, the smell of cheap disinfectant and memory ink overpowering the dingy room.

"Please indicate with your fingers, pincers, or tentacles where you would like the patch to go and remove all clothing, hair, or fur from the surrounding area." the robot says, their one eye following my pointer finger to the base of my spine. With a smirk, my beloved unzips my dress and pulls it down to my waist. She offers me no second guesses or questions, just a hand on the back of my head as I lean forward, cradled on her shoulder.

"Commencing in three, two, one—"

The Memory Ink's needle flits across my back this way and that as every whispered slur, bad date, and fucked up memory slips through my brain like sand through a sieve. One last pinch and we're home free, all my hurt patched away, inked deep into my skin, pain replaced with unbridled joy.

"Where do you wanna go now?" She asks from her captain's chair.

As long as it's with her, anywhere.

LYDIA'S BACK

JAMES DUNHAM (300 WORDS)

Honorable Mention

When the rescue vessel's archivist came, Lydia hunched in her quarters and crossed her arms, shy.

"I know it still hurts," said the archivist. "We can chat first if that makes you comfortable."

Lydia didn't meet her eyes. The archivist's umber face was striking, and Lydia couldn't bear beauty just then. "No, it's fine."

Lydia took off her shirt, displaying her pale, acned back now blue with tattoo. How much data these symbols preserved was unguessable—there'd been no time for tests. If Celeste hadn't thought of tattoos, the malware would have destroyed everything. Lydia's skin still burned from the ink apparatus's thousand simultaneous microcuts. Whenever she closed her eyes she saw the station recede into space, lights dying, smoke. A century-old community reduced to pods ejecting like wreckage.

The archivist scanned the tattoo. "Beautiful, thank you."

Lydia put on her shirt. "Can you read it?"

"Not before decompression—the key takes up five people's backs. We don't know whose yet." She touched Lydia's arm. "Don't worry. Whatever you chose to take with you, you'll get it. I promise."

Lydia shrunk from her touch. "Okay."

"Anything else you'd like archived? I can record things. You talk my ear off, I listen. Think of your future self. What would she want to remember?"

Lydia's mouth felt dry. Her back held the one thing she'd wanted—the holo of Liam and Flora and her, the year they'd all been lovers.

What could she say to encompass the wholeness she'd given her home?

46

No speech could suffice.

Lydia took from her locker a shirt stained with blood. "When I got tattooed... I bled for my station. I'd do it again."

The archivist scanned the stained shirt. Recorded Lydia's words. "Nothing more?"

Lydia looked at the woman's waiting eyes. "Nothing an archive could hold."

SIGNED

AMANDA CHERRY (300 WORDS)

"Sign Here."

Declan is terrified.

But why?

Isn't this the goal: work magic so powerful as to garner the attention of the Manor Sorceress, pledge fealty, and live out life happily in her employ?

Yes. It's what Declan has always wanted.

So why is putting pen to page so frightening?

"Here?" Declan asks, pointing to the only blank space on the parchment.

"There," the Sorceress replies. Her arms are crossed over her chest; she's noticed Declan's hesitation. "You wouldn't be the first to turn down this deal," she says. "But be warned: this is a one-time offer. You leave this place without having signed, and you may never return."

Declan nods.

It's now or never.

A dip of quill into ink, a scratching of nib upon parchment. It's done.

But something feels off. Wrong. Declan is confused.

"What is this?" the Sorceress snaps. "You dare attempt to deceive me?" She snatches the page from the table. Orange flames dance in her eyes as the heat of her wrath fills the room.

She's furious.

Declan is afraid again.

"What? No!"

"Then why do you sign a false name?"

"I didn't!"

"I will not abide lies!" The Sorceress slams the contract back onto the table. "This is magic," she snarls. "It requires your *true* name."

Declan stops short. She couldn't mean….

"My true…"

"Yes."

"Kadeene?"

Kadeene is Declan's secret, inner self.

No one has ever spoken her name aloud before.

"That is your true name, isn't it?"

Declan gapes, then smiles.

"My… true name."

Kadeene dips quill into ink again. This time nib meets parchment without fear. Kadeene feels the magic descend upon her; it's warm and heady. It tastes sweet. Her lips and fingers tingle.

The deal is struck.

True name and true self: now bound in ink and by magic.

SUBVERSION
SARA TESTAROSSA (300 WORDS)

Last week, Zhenya knew three truths about soulmates:

- Soultech's tattoos guarantee finding one's soulmate.
- She doesn't want a soulmate.
- Therefore, something's fundamentally wrong with her.

Today, after shifting paradigms, she knows only one is true.
The one that means she's ok, though most of the world disagrees.
For now.

ZHENYA CHOSE a discreet government mandated Soultat, ostensibly because of her Judaism. Though all faiths embraced Soultats, many people did similar, in deference to tradition. Too unsettled by the truth, she secretly pretended hers was a beauty mark. Visualizing ink-suspended nanobots analyzing her genome, changing accordingly, preparing to tingle when near another's compatible nanobots, hurt more than the needle.

Though happy for any friend finding their soulmate, Zhenya never understood the natural progression of soulmates supplanting friends. She dreaded meeting hers, but hid this; she should be excited, not feel ill.

Then Zhenya found the Subversives. Meeting people in such varied relationships—some with soulmates, some not, some in multiple relationships —was eye-opening. The biggest shock and relief was Ari, whose soulmate was their best friend, not the "most compatible romantic and sexual partner" Soultech advertised. Ari, whose feelings mirrored hers, assured her she wasn't broken.

Zhenya was buffeted by a whirlwind of emotions while learning terms long suppressed worldwide—asexual, aromantic, polyamorous—nonconforming identities that threatened corporate control.

Ari suggested she take time to decide whether to join their fight. The community welcomed anyone like-minded, but undermining Soultech required active dissidents.

She agreed to think it over, but already knew her answer.

THE NANOBOTS in Zhenya's tattoo remain dormant; no tingling in her inked skin indicates anything's changed. But so much has.

She knows the world's wrong, not her.

For the first time, Zhenya feels how Soultech says she should with her soulmate: unconditionally accepted.

Among fellow Subversives, she's home.

PARANORMAL PART ONE

"We can all be better than we've heretofore dreamed. Our potential is unlimited as long as we're not functioning from the negative."

— L.A. BANKS, *SHADOW WALKER*

DEVIL AND ADVOCATES

KIM FIELDING (299 WORDS)

"No use having regrets now," the Devil said, waving the parchment. "You signed the contract, fair and square."

Erica looked at her corpse, cooling on the bed between them. The hospital staff had disconnected the tubes and machines, and she supposed they'd soon wheel the body away to the morgue, where Jade's earthly remains waited. "I thought we'd live longer," she sighed.

"I promised you peace and happiness with your wife. You had that for eleven years. My end of the bargain is done. I'll take your soul now." The Devil glanced at his Apple Watch impatiently.

"But an airplane engine crashed through our bedroom ceiling!" They'd been so careful about eating right and exercising. What good were all those kale smoothies now?

"Not my doing. Look, this is your signature in your blood. Your soul belongs to me." The Devil tried an evil laugh but broke off, coughing.

Erica steeled herself and wondered if she could manage some union organizing in Hell.

The Devil held out a clawed hand. "Let's go. We're—"

"Not so fast!"

Erica screeched with joyous surprise and gave her ghostly wife a hug. Jade looked damned gorgeous for a dead woman.

Jade smiled at the Devil. "You can't have her soul. There's a prior claim. Mine. She gave me her soul the day we got engaged." She had sharper teeth now than when she was alive; Erica was sure of it. "You should have done your due diligence before offering a contract. Conducted a title search, maybe."

Smoke poured from the Devil's ears, and his parchment poofed into ashes. "This isn't fair!" he wailed.

Erica spared one last glance for the despondent Devil. "You should be careful when dealing with lawyers." She took Jade's hand, and together they walked into the blinding light.

THE AUTOGRAPH

TAM AMES (298 WORDS)

Honorable Mention

Andrea stood in the dark near the back door of the theatre, waiting, her hand wrapped around the pen in her pocket. She had nothing but time now that Trini was dead. When a stagehand came out for a cigarette, he blocked open the door and Andrea slipped inside. She'd been here before; she knew where she was going. Third door on the left.

Merilee Weathers sat on the couch, script in hand. She looked up when the door opened. Her crystal blue eyes widened slightly at the sight of Andrea, her gaze moved down Andrea's body, soft pink lips parting. As Merilee's gaze heated, the raw magnetism of the woman made Andrea understand Trini's choice. The woman was beautiful… and deadly.

Merilee licked her lips, "Can I help you, my pretty?"

Andrea lowered her eyes, "I'm a big fan. I was hoping for your autograph." She pulled out a playbill and the pen filled with green ink.

"Just an autograph?" Merilee came closer.

"What else?" Andrea suppressed the growl that rose in her throat at her approach.

"Well, we'll see, won't we?"

As she put the pen to paper and scrawled her name, Andrea watched the green ink turn red, the proof. It was like blood, like Trini's blood that this witch had bathed in.

Merilee looked at Andrea, perfectly arched brows raised.

Andrea held her gaze, fangs descending. Before Merilee could raise her hand to grasp the charm around her neck, her impossibly young neck for a

95-year-old woman, Andrea whispered, "For Trini." And struck. The blood red ink was soon obscured by the real thing.

She slipped back outside gripping the pen in her pocket. "For you my love. It's over now." While the centuries ahead looked no less bleak, revenge had its own rewards.

UNMOORED
MEGHAN BYERS (287 WORDS)

"Does it help?" Eva asks, tracing the lines of ink on Carmen's forearm. A tree, branches fanning out toward the inside of Carmen's elbow, roots stretching toward her wrist. *An anchor*, Carmen had called it. "Does it stay? When you change?"

"I don't know," Carmen answers. "I can't tell, when I'm..." She trails off, still unwilling to say it plainly despite Eva's knowledge, and despite her own: that she could be any shape, any creature, and Eva still would love her.

"Too much fur," Eva guesses, lips quirked in a smile.

It's not that, really. It's the wolf's eyes, pointed always forward, the wolf's nose, parsing the language of scent. The wolf's mind, uninterested in such terribly human questions.

"Yes," Carmen says anyway, leaning in to kiss Eva, hand on her cheek, soft and sweet in a way she didn't know she knew how to be.

LATER, when her bones stretch and rearrange, when the agony overwhelms her, Carmen tries, for just a flickering moment, to catch a glimpse of the tattoo. But she can't see anything. She can only feel, ache, be.

In the wolf's body she is more present than she has ever been. In the wolf's body she knows everything.

"I SHOULD GET ONE. A tattoo. Matching," Eva says after one full moon night, lying in bed beside Carmen, who is wolf-worn and bone-weary, barely able to open her eyes.

She does open them, though. And says, "Why?"

Eva smiles at her with a fondness that shouldn't be possible. Of all the impossible things Carmen has been, to be loved now, is—

Eva touches her forearm very lightly to Carmen's, obscuring branches with skin. A warm, barely-there weight.

She says, "An anchor."

INKED

JEFF RONAN (293 WORDS)

The sex is good, largely because it's so unexpected.

Peter had chatted me up in line at Chipotle, his nice-boy smirk framed by almost comically tousled blonde hair. In the same breath, he told me I had beautiful eyes and made fun of my scuffed sneakers. I could have jumped him right there.

"What's all this?" he asks afterwards in bed, tracing a finger across one of my tattoos: *Annie* splashed across my right hip in a spidery, lavender scrawl. There's an inch of space separating the 'e' from another tattoo, the name *Johnny* running down my thigh in aggressive, blocky letters.

"It's my ink," I shrug.

He grins. "No shit. What do they mean?"

In all, there are eighteen tattoos scattered across my body, each one a different first name. I always tell people they're for singers I love: 'Jeff' for Buckley, 'Tina' for Turner, etc. It's easier than the truth.

"Well?" Peter asks, his fingers travelling inward. I feel my cock stiffen under his touch, and I kiss him instead of answering.

I ASK him if he wants to stay longer, but he says he has somewhere to be, a friend's birthday out in Bushwick. One last kiss and he's gone, his unfinished Chipotle cold on the counter.

Before I can wonder when I'll see him again, I feel a warmth prickling against my ribs. I tug my t-shirt off, watching as the new tattoo forms, Seurat-like, dot by dot.

I sigh. I've never known why the names show up, only that when they do, it means I've seen the last of their possessor. I frown as the tattoo finishes taking shape: the name *Casey* in neat, black cursive.

I wonder if the number he gave me was fake too.

THE MIDNIGHT LIBRARIAN

ORION O'CONNELL (286 WORDS)

Dark and muddled is the ink vining up their arms.

Names like poison, sinister, deadly, caught in the book summoning itself at *its* whim, never at theirs. They are merely the guardian, the keeper. Ghost is the librarian, living the cold existence of their own name.

Breath catches and causes them to shudder. They're gonna be all right, just gotta stay grounded 'till it passes. The book calls. The souls of the lost know their name. The fingerprints left by the *otherness* stain, but do not leave bruises. Ghost's jar of souls will disappear quickly as it comes, locked away forever, until they join with the others one day.

Such is the price. One does not collect the souls of the wicked without becoming such. When this is over, their hands will not be stained with blood, but with ink.

As it should be.

Defeat. One blink and the nothingness grows.

Eyes open to a new world, a new identity with the careful illusion of *'safe'*. And there's Annie, beautiful Annie, smiling down on them as they stare out the window at the gray London sky.

"You look like you haven't been sleeping again."

Maybe they'll ask her out this time. But what's the point? What's ever the point? Which world is the real one, which is the fake? Who is to say? If they choose wrongly, if they spend too much time in one...

We're all doomed.

Ghost thinks back to a Shakespeare quote: 'hell is empty, and all the devils are here.'

Doesn't exactly make for a restful night's sleep.

And there are worse things still, waiting just under their skin.
The book. Imprinted on them.
Like ink, like a tattoo.
Unyielding, unresting.
Searching.

FLUID
BRYAN CRYSTAL-THURSTON (299 WORDS)

Honorable Mention

JUDGE'S CHOICE - B.A. Brock

I'd just absorbed a meal of socks and some cat hair when little Grayson Conifer called out in the night. "Dad!"

An elder human's feet appeared beneath the bed. "What's wrong?"

"The monster."

I cursed myself for eating too loud.

"Let me check."

I expected them to do as they always did: to look upon my amorphous maw and conflate darkness with emptiness. "There's nothing there," they'd say.

Except, this face was different from the one called "Dad"—more hair in less places. "Oh! Hello, Mr. Monster!"

I rippled. I'd been seen many times but never recognized. I'd nearly found my voice when they spoke for me.

"He says, 'Hello.' Will you say, 'hello,' back?"

"Hello," Grayson said.

The elder turned their ear to me. "What's that? Mmhmm. Absolutely!" They stood. "Mr. Monster wants you to know, there's nothing to worry about. He—"

I hissed. I couldn't stop myself.

The elder faltered but continued. "He just wants a cozy place to sleep, but he says—"

"They." I congealed. I almost never congeal.

"What?" the elder asked Grayson.

"*They*," I repeated.

The elder's face appeared beneath the bed again, slowly. "Hello?"

"Hello," I answered for myself this time.

"W-w-who are you?"

As the elder pulled away from me, I followed, a shivering, fluid mass of ink. My tendrils wrapped around the bedframe and hauled my darkness into the moonlight. "Of all the things I am, I am not 'he'."

The elder's eyes grew wide. Silence hung between us.

It was Grayson that spoke first. "You made them sad, Mommy. You have to say you're sorry."

Mommy looked at Grayson, then at me. "S-sorry."

"Thank you."

"What would you like to be called?"

It took me a moment to answer little Grayson. No one had ever asked. "Call me... 'Friend'."

Every year, judging for the Queer Sci Fi Flash Fiction Anthology contest feels as if I'm coming back to old friends, and every year I'm delighted to make new ones. My new friend this year is the story Fluid, my judge's pick, which coincidentally is also about friendship. The main character, a gender nonconforming amorphous monster, is maybe a touch too relatable to me: definitely awkward, a bit cranky, and possibly lonely. The endearing protagonist combined with the engaging dialog and the sweet Monsters Inc. vibe compelled me to elevate this story in our publication, and I'm deeply grateful for its representation. As always, it's been a pleasure. See you next year.

—Ben Brock

WRITER'S BLOOD

ARON CAER (300 WORDS)

Layla soaked every page, swollen eyes reading the words until they were all her aching heart contained. They were Danni's last words, written between cherished moments. The drunk driver didn't care that she hated to leave a story unfinished.

Danni's story had abruptly ended. All that remained were blank pages and memories. The blood had long since dried, almost as black as the ink of her pen, the words hastily scrawled during her last breath.

I love you, Layla.

Layla's sobs softened to steady breaths as sleep took her. Within tenebrous dreams, Danni's pen wrote tales of lovers in a sea of dark seductions. When Layla awoke, she found that ink and tears were bleeding out of the pages.

The ink oozed over her hand, slowly consuming her like an undulating, hungry mouth. Layla screamed, struggling to wipe away the black ichor only to spread it further on her skin. It seeped through her clothes, coating every inch of quivering flesh.

Fear heightened Layla's senses, making her intimately aware of the fluid's creeping. She gasped at the flood of intense sensations, the ooze finding its way between her thighs. A finger's caress, the swirl of a tongue, fueled by passions that only one person could ignite.

"D-Danni?"

Layla tasted the salty kiss of lips, ebony and wet. She allowed herself to become immersed in the sticky ink, form and formless fingers interlacing in the penumbral flow. She understood now why Danni came back, the beautiful writer unable to leave a story unfinished.

Between the empty pages of the book, Layla's body became the ink Danni needed to finish their story.

Lovers embrace in every written letter. Every word telling a song of passions in the dark…

And in the ink of every sentence, flows a symphonic harmony, two as one.

OFF THE WALL

AINSLIE LLOYD (300 WORDS)

Giselle blinked.

Blinked? After two centuries frozen? A miracle! Her parched eyes rejoiced. Blood flowed; dusty flatness plumped. The picture frame no longer held her.

Giselle tumbled onto the bed. Where *le cochon* neglected *sa femme, la pauvre chère,* every night. *Que terrible,* to always see from the wall!

Returned to her full size, Giselle shuddered. *Ink!* First, *l'artiste vicieux* who'd ogled as he painted, then used her body, again, again... Writing his name upon her ankle! Now – *merde!* More black markings! From *le cochon.*

In the room for washing, she could hear water – *la chère,* whose name she never heard. *L'homme* was always gone, returning late, sweating angry whisky fumes. She must wash off the cursed ink!

Giselle could not sit up.

La chère entered and looked from Giselle to the picture frame, now aslant. Though her mouth opened, no sound came.

"Please." So hard to speak this odd language! "Please, I may wash?" She indicated her dusty breasts, the ink stains. "I cannot get up." *Merde! To lie forever on this bed...?*

La chère chewed her lip. *Oh,* to kiss that mouth! "I'll help." Her voice spoke curious caution, while covering her nakedness with a sheet.

She brought basin and cloths. Gentle hands washed her feet. Giselle sighed at the blessing of a woman's touch. As the ink came off her ankle, her foot moved. *"Merci! Merci!"* She sat up. "I finish."

In the washing room, Giselle scrubbed the remaining ink stains from her skin. And wept.

"How can I help?" A towel came around her, a warm body held her, until the tears slowed.

Giselle dried her face. "We leave here? Together?"

La chère stepped back. Giselle could not guess her thoughts.

"Je m'appelle Giselle," she said. *"Et toi?"*

La chère smiled, then laughed. "Gabi," she said.

UNTITLED

S. A. HUNT (300 WORDS)

"Kick ass and take names," Frank says over the register. "Nice ink."

"Life motto," the tall girl replies in a husky rasp.

Her violin figure is sinuous under a tank top and jeans, and the waistband of a black thong peeks over the rise of each hip. Her upper lip bears the ghost-stain of a mustache. Every square inch—except for her face and fingers—is covered in words; several hundred, in scrawling cursive.

Names.

Ring-a-ding! A man walks into the Pay-and-Tote.

City cop, black uniform. Beefy, acne-scarred. Name pin says *Ofc. Howard.* A nightly regular. He takes a bag of Combos and gets in line.

"What do I owe you?" she asks.

Pall Malls and Jägermeister. "Twenty-seven fifty-one."

"Here." She hands Frank a twenty and a ten.

"New in town?" Howard asks her. "Thought I saw you down by Fifth. Cool tattoos. What's your name, son?" Cold, hard eyes. They flick downwards.

"I don't have a name," says the girl.

"No?" Howard bares his teeth in a robotic smile.

"Still looking for one."

He turns to face her, putting his Combos on the counter. "Marlboro Reds, please." To the girl, "Plannin' on drinkin' that Jäger on the way home, boy?"

"No."

"Dressed awful cute tonight. There a reason you're walking?"

"I ain't got a car."

"That so?" One heavy hand on her shoulder. "Wait here. I wanna talk to you in a minute."

Frank rings up his purchase.

"What's your name?" asks the girl.

"Mine?" Howard points at his name tag.

"No, your first name."

"Danny. You gettin' familiar?"

Taking a fountain pen out of her pocket, the girl writes *Danny Howard* on her left elbow. "Thanks."

"For what?" says a man in a cop uniform. Frank has never seen him before.

"Good night." The girl exits, stage right.

HOW TO CREATE A MONSTER

APRIL KELLEY (287 WORDS)

Recipe:
> Ink
> One magic pen
> Your heart's intention.

INSTRUCTIONS:
> Focus on your intention.
> Dip pen into ink.
> Write.

THE RECIPE HADN'T SEEMED SO difficult upon having the conversation with the witch. The day of the performance was upon him, and Harper's nerves got the better of him. His hands shook as he held the pen above the inkwell.

Focusing on his intention proved to be the easiest part. He'd pictured himself standing on his balcony, watching his monster exact revenge. High society and their filthy gossip killed his lover and he wanted to make them pay.

He dipped the pen into the ink, expecting some hint of magic, but none came. It wasn't until the pen's tip touched paper that dark magic swirled like smoke.

His hand moved as if it had a mind all its own, writing his intention. He sucked in a breath and held it. A lump formed in his throat and his chest ached. He gave his lungs a reprieve when tears fell.

Eleazar.

When did grief stop and healing begin?

Eleazar lifted off the parchment. The letters blended into a black mass. Harper scrambled out of his chair, his back hitting the shelves behind him. Air, entering and exiting his body, was all he heard.

The mass took shape. Limbs and a male chest. Ink turned to naked flesh. Harper knew that body well.

Eleazar.

Eleazar flexed his fingers and then traced the scars on his wrists.

"Eleazar." Their gazes met. Harper held out a shaky hand. Would he turn to vapor?

Eleazar closed the distance, cupping Harper's cheek. His palm felt cool against his skin.

"My heart's intention was to create a monster."

When Eleazar smiled, he flashed fangs. "You did."

I NEVER KNEW

EYTAN BERNSTEIN (300 WORDS)

JUDGE'S CHOICE - KA Masters

Our parents named you Link. You always thought that was hilarious. You always said, "I'm no hero, Zelda. That's you."

My twin, my best friend, you were, you are, you will always be—my hero.

When I came out, you hugged me. You were shaking, and I was worried you disapproved.

When the kids at school bullied me and called me a dyke, you stopped them.

I thought you were an ally. I never knew what was happening inside you—I should have.

The triforce inked on my wrist was missing one piece, the piece inked on you. You held my hand while the needle marked us.

You recognized the rainbow that was sparkling in me, was sparkling in you too. I never knew how hard that was for you.

You hid your pain behind your jokes, behind your dedication, behind your love. I should have seen the signs.

Three days ago, you took your life. One bottle of pills and you never woke up. I didn't see it coming.

In the letter you left me, you poured out your grief in ink and tears. You wished you'd been as brave as me, wished you'd come out when I did, wished you'd cared less about what people thought of you.

I thought the world of you, you asshole! And that wouldn't have changed when you opened the closet door. You should have let me be your big sister, let me cry with you, not over you.

Your funeral was over, but I lingered at your grave, holding onto your soul. In the deepening darkness, I glimpsed your spirit for but a moment, reaching out to me. And when you touched me, my wrist glowed, the triforce sparkling, complete—one final gift to me from you.

And then you were gone.

Despite the gut-wrenching sad tone of the submission, I adored "I Never Knew." The bond between the siblings felt incredibly authentic, and the devastating consequences of suicide in the piece highlight the ongoing need to support our LGBTQIA+ youth.

—KA Masters

FANTASY PART TWO

"This is magic we're talking about. It's supposed to go places science can't, defy logic, wink at technology, fill us all with the sense of wonder that comes of gazing upon a fictional world and seeing something truly different from our own."

— N.K. Jemisin

ON THE CONJOINED PRACTICE OF DEMONOLOGY AND SCRIBAL LONGHAND

K. EASON (299 WORDS)

Ketje's skin flushes as Donye's clever fingers thread around her. Together, they grip the quill.

"Upstroke here, pressure like *so*." Donye's lips are cold (why are they cold?) on Ketje's ear.

Oh. There is no breath to warm them.

On Ketje's own (warm) lips to ask why—

But then she wakes, and remembers.

THE ABBOT WAITS in the scriptorium, flanked by the janissaries, holding the quill on outstretched palms: an offering. The janissaires hold their swords: threat and promise.

Ketje's trial manuscript waits on the table (only threat): *Three Monsters,* with its crabbed, fussy script that initiates dread, that monks mutter about.

The third line is the worst, those runes!

Also on the table: Virgin vellum, for *her* attempt. Her copy must be flawless. *Flawless*, or--

Or.

Blood stains the table, faded black, newer red. Donye is not the first failure. Will not be the last.

Ketje takes the quill. Jabs the nib into inkwell. Ink ripples on the surface. And under her skin, an ominous roiling as her demon wakes. All scribes are possessed--to wield a quill at all is invitation. But scribes who fail their test, who can't control their demon, *become* the demon. And then the janissaires strike them dead.

Ketje draws the nib out, taps it clean, touches the vellum. Writes the first letter, smooth and fearless. The second, third. *Perfect* inking.

The demon sparks under her skin. Fiery filaments thread her nerves, burn under the flesh.

She expected cold. (The scriptoriums are, always). Expected stiff and clumsy fingers to smear the ink. She had practiced against that.

But this heat feels like Donye, fingers wrapped through Ketje's. Sweat slicks her (their?) hand, slicks the quill.

Like so, Donye whispers in her ear. Only this time, her breath is hot.

Their fingers slip.

THE SKINCHANGER'S ART
RE ANDEEN (290 WORDS)

Jaro inked Elya's likeness into his chest, right over his heart. His childhood love, now property of the Tyrant. Pigment met blood and Jaro *became* Elya, slave-marked from ears to ankles.

Strolling into the Keep, as if returning from market, Jaro-Elya hid a sly grin. The Tyrant was invulnerable to high wizardry, but against the lowly skinchanger's art, he was defenseless.

A disabled guard, a purloined uniform, and three inky skinchanges later, Jaro stood before the Obsidian Ring, vessel of the Tyrant's power. The evil thing was encased in a vortex of eldritch energy; its touch was death.

Jaro leaned over the vortex—carefully! —extending a pinky downward. He inked scales and a forked tongue, then fell into the swirling eye. His sleek serpentine form arrowed through the Ring, curled around it, and the spell was broken. The Ring shattered, and with it all the Tyrant's sorcery.

The Self that hit the floor was Jara, the girl he never wanted to be, but she had no time to sort herself. She ran for the roof, the Keep quaking underfoot.

Feathers inked on outstretched hands soared upward, high over Varyat Bay. Golden eyes spotted the safehouse, and Jaro-eagle dove, back-winged, then all went black.

~

ELYA LOOKED on Jaro like a stranger.

"Jara?" Recognition bloomed. "Is that really you?"

"I promised I'd free you." Jaro took her in his arms.

"So you did." Elya leaned back, examining his angular, masculine form. Her slave-marks gone, she glowed. "But ... *how*?"

"Does it matter?"

"No." Elya smiled up at him. "All that matters is we're together, whatever your shape."

He pulled her close. "Always."

Elya laid her cheek against his chest, skin on skin. Not the skin of his birth; the skin he chose.

THE MARKS OF A KNIGHT

ADA MARIA SOTO (274 WORDS)

The air was damn near toxic with Sharpie fumes and the felt tip tickled as it was swirled around her lower back.

"Is it really necessary to draw on my ass?" The drag of the pen was briefly replaced with a kiss on her tailbone.

"You are going into battle my love. I will give you every drop of protection I can."

"The fumes are going to kill me before any raider or dark mage."

"Stop complaining. You've got the best witch in town literally covering your ass here. And Sharpie sticks a hell of a lot better than lampblack and gum. Now hold still."

Sir Tressa closed her eyes and let Margot continue her work. The other knights of the city would be going through the same preparations. Checking their swords and rifles and being prepared by their witches. Some had magic carved into their armor. Others had it carved into their skin. Tressa preferred this despite the tickle and the smell. The magic would stay the length of the battle and break with a good scrub, letting her feel human again.

Already she could feel the magic strengthening her muscles and quickening her nerves. Soon it would also begin to deaden her emotions until there was nothing left but the need for battle and a clarity of purpose.

"Wait." Margot had begun to draw across her chest, a final sigil to link all the magic in place. "Before it no longer occurs to me to say this, I love you. Be safe. I'll see you on the battlements."

Margot gave her a kiss. "My brave, sweet knight. I love you too."

THE INK READER

RYAN BREADINC (267 WORDS)

Honorable Mention

The Ink Reader's office is empty of visitors.

"There aren't many young ones who can afford this service."

The receptionist snatches away the golden coins nonetheless, the shine of them obscured by the green-inked skin of her hands. She counts them out one by one, taking more than the fee advertised. It doesn't matter.

"You can sit down now, sir," she adds without looking up.

Maybe this was a bad idea.

A nearby door slams open, a man with arching red lines up his face and throat stalking out. He's muttering to himself in an angry tone, curses and swears in a bitter voice. Whatever he has been told his fate is, it can't have been anything good. He looks as if he's ready to murder someone.

"It's all bullshit!" he snarls as he heads for the exit. "Don't listen to whatever they tell you, boy."

The receptionist pays no attention to the man's outburst. "Some people don't like the truth. Sit down."

A few minutes pass, and the anxiety begins to creep in.

The receptionist gets up and leaves.

The waiting room feels enormous with only one person to fill the space. Waiting is painful.

What if this was a mistake?

"The Ink Reader is ready for you."

A person appears in the doorway.

The only word fit for them is *beautiful* – no other description fits, not

84

even one that might suggest gender or identity other than something other-worldly and all-knowing, and they smile through red-painted lips, leaning up against the doorway.

"Hello, young lady," the Ink Reader says, and she begins to cry with relief.

INDELIBLE INK
TOSHI DRAKE (300 WORDS)

Standing on the edge of the clearing was painful. I was awkward and out of place among the fae with their endless energy and beautiful everything. But Rowan insisted and I didn't have the energy or capability to say no to them. I never could say no.

Rowan moved fluidly, their body undulating to the rhythm of the music. They were lost to everything but music in their head; I was entranced by the look of sheer joy radiating from them.

I stepped into the clearing, drawn by their exuberance, desperate to know what they felt.

Their skin was marked with bright images of stars and moons. Every tattoo a clue to who they were. Their hair, a waterfall of colours cascading down their back, made my hands twitch, needing to feel the satin against them.

I had never felt this longing before and then I met Rowan. They were butterflies on top of slithery snakes as I dealt with these overwhelming feelings of excitement and dread.

How could one explain what this was? What does it mean when your breath catches when the person you love smiles at you?

Rowan was imprinted on me. They were an indelible ink on my soul. Their joy, a bright tattoo of colours, shouting to everyone who saw, I was worth it.

I bit my lip wondering what I could do, my eyes meeting the kind and knowing eyes. They left their partner and moved toward me with purpose. They were determined to make me happy. They would say everything with the brightness of their smile.

They would know without asking. They would take me in their arms and embrace me. And that would be my moment, my time in the sun and I could know what it meant to be loved.

LIVENAME

ANNA STACY (300 WORDS)

Callista found the apellomancer on her first try. Their house was small, of stone, nearly buried in the trees, so covered in ivy that it could have been a hill. The door fell open when she knocked.

The apellomancer was sitting on the floor. They looked up and sniffed the air.

"You already have a name," they said. "Why are you here?"

Callista nodded. "I do," she confirmed. She twisted the hem of her skirt. "I just want people to use it."

The apellomancer's eyes blazed. "Who does not respect your name?"

Callista traced a circle in the dirt with a toe. "Oh," she said. "A lot of people."

They rose, swifter than Callista had thought possible, and strode across the cottage. Callista watched, not daring to move as the apellomancer pulled a tome out of the dark clay of the wall.

"Your name is Callista," they said, producing a plume from their sleeve. A beetle crawled across the open book; the apellomancer snatched it up and ground it between two fingers. "And so you must be called."

They dipped the feather into the beetle's ink and drew.

"I don't have much money," Callista put in as the apellomancer tore out the page and folded it small.

"Here," they said. "Eat this."

Callista hesitated. "What is it?"

The apellomancer smiled. "It's you."

Callista closed her eyes and placed it on her tongue. And there, the word bloomed: her very own name, and it was right, and good, and hers.

Callista made it out of the woods on her first try. She went straight to her uncle's store, her stomach all in knots.

"Well," he said. "If it isn't Callista."

She grinned.

He frowned. "Not Callista. I meant to say Callista."

Callista smiled. Her name was right, and good, and hers.

HE BLEEDS INK
CHARLIE BOYNTON (300 WORDS)

Kitsch bleeds ink.

That's what he tells everyone when they see his night-touched fingers and the dark smears on his brow that drift into his hairline. He scrubs away the stains left behind from a young woman he once saw in the mirror. Sometimes they fade into a light dusting, but they never wash away, not really.

The ink is obvious and loud in every way that Kitsch isn't. It's an answer to an equation that he doesn't want anyone to know he's trying to solve. It's a sign to an attraction he doesn't want anyone to see.

Rewriting oneself is messy business. It means taking apart the old, analyzing it, and learning what's actually his and what's not. Outlines of a life lived by someone he no longer knows scatter across his desk at night. Thoughts written on notes and napkins are connected by pins and strings like he's looking for a creature lost to a legend in a long-abandoned forest.

Tonight, Kitsch's stained hands don't earn his ire. He doesn't scrub away a mark that found its way under his eye. For the first time, he looks at his work, the reworked revelations, and planned pages for a future he hopes is for him, and he understands.

The ink isn't punishment or revenge from a ghost of a girl. It's a trophy. Evidence of time spent knowing who he is and what he wants. His ink represents his dedication to himself and a community that is ready to welcome him with open, similarly ink-stained arms.

Most of all, it's the backbone of the blueprint to his joy.

So, Kitsch doesn't actually *bleed* ink. He wears it proudly on his skin, his clothes, his cheeks when he smiles, untouched and celebrated.

Just as all joy and euphoria should be.

INKSHADER

TAYLOR RAMAGE (293 WORDS)

New lead, new city. Doors slam shut as if I have *any* interest in robbing their shops. But when *I* come around, it's to handle their greatest "problem."

My Inkshade senses the new, unconcentrated magic and leads me to a Ruva woman. Pierced, pointed ears. Disheveled, purple hair. Two Ruva men–her brothers, maybe–scowl, tightening the ropes binding her hands. I'm sick of people constantly misunderstanding Sketchlings. This woman can't *use* her magic in any meaningful way, not until I do my work.

"How long will this take?" One man demands.

His hostile tone grates me, but such is the life of an Inkshader. "A few minutes. I need her arms free."

Once they untie her, they shove her to the ground. "You overpowered perverts can keep her."

I kneel at her side and take the Inkshade pen from my pouch. "Which arm?"

No answer.

"Left it is, then," I say gently. As I work, my Inkshade guides me in filling her Sketch. The magic within her swells to color the spot. "This will let you use it. People will leave you alone when they see it. If they don't, well, you know how *effective* Inkshade is."

"I shouldn't have asked her to dinner," the woman's voice shakes. "I thought she…had that inclination. But she told the whole city and…"

"You're never certain until you see a woman bearing Inkshade. But if she's pretty, you get your Sketch anyway," I sigh as I pull the pen away from her completed mark, a soft, violet flower.

Her frown remains.

"Yes, most everyone hates us. Inkshaders protect each other, though. Come stay safe with us." I extend my hand. After a moment's hesitation, she takes it.

One more for our family against the world.

THE DRAGON'S PRICE

M.K. MADS (294 WORDS)

Honorable Mention

An old man crept from the cave's shadows. "You wish to bargain for the power of the dragon."

El clutched her sword's pommel and met his sharp gaze. "I do."

Dangerous, the village elders had said. To bind with a dragon was to sacrifice something dear. Her mother had begged her not to, but as the village guardian, El had to do *something* before the encroaching army reached them.

The old man gave a toothless grin. "Then you must give of yourself."

El set her jaw. "I'm aware. What is the price?"

"You must give up your love for another."

El blinked. "Come again?"

He pointed one gnarled finger at the tattooed pattern on her left hand that marked her as wed. "The love you feel for the wife you've chosen. That is the price the dragon demands."

"Ah." El tapped her sword. "This would be the *romantic* love, yes?"

The old man cackled. "Of course. What other kind is there that would bind you to a wife?"

"Just checking." El nodded firmly. "It helps to be clear when one is making bargains, don't you agree?"

His toothless grin returned. "Indeed."

"Very well," El said. "I accept the dragon's price to protect my village."

The old man laughed, a light flashed, and El knew no more.

~

SHARI MET her at the edge of the village and gasped over the black scales inked along El's right arm, all the way up the side of her neck to her face. "It's done?"

El nodded. "It's done."

Shari threw her arms around her. "What price did you pay?"

El laughed to herself and hugged her partner tightly; the warm feelings she had were not diminished, for this love had never been romantic. "Nothing I would miss."

HIDDEN SPELL

NICOLE DENNIS (299 WORDS)

"Univ-Date 0681-3531. Location: Earth. Drone survey indicated intact metal depression," Darijo Carinaka said. "Located steel door."

An unlocking click echoed. The door disappeared into a slit. LED lights flickered.

"A Faraday cage?"

Only a wooden desk stood inside.

Activating an air spray to remove the dust layer, Darijo discovered hidden items. There was a quill pen – a swan feather with a nib fashioned from the shaft. A scroll was kept open by an ink bottle and covered with mystical symbols and a phrase:

To reveal what is hidden
Draw an infinity loop
Speak: 'Leonardo, my love, return to me'

Darijo removed the bottle's stopper and swirled the ink. Something sparkled within the abyss. He twirled the pen and dipped the nib. He drew an infinity loop underneath the lower symbols. Then he spoke the words.

Nothing happened.

Disappointed, Darijo turned to leave.

A shimmer glowed and brightened. The ink sparkled while it lifted from the scroll. It swirled into a spiral. With a burst, it dissipated throughout.

A metamorphopsia appearance spread. Objects emerged – cabinets, bed, bathroom corner, mini-kitchen.

A human coalesced from translucence to solid. He wore jeans, shirt, and shoes. His dark green eyes widened. "Who are you? What are you? Herman?"

Darijo released his helmet into his exo-suit. It disclosed his uniqueness –

golden skin, white hair, pale eyes. "I'm Darijo, a Rijinian exo-explorer. Are you Leonardo? Who is Herman?"

"Yes. He's my ex. He locked me in here, in a stasis. Of sorts. What happened?"

"Destruction of Earth. Global warming. Solar radiation. All Terrans left."

"Terrans?"

"Humans."

"What year is it?"

"3531."

Leonardo paled. "1500 years."

"Unbelievable."

"I have papers to prove it. You freed me."

"What do you want?"

"Can you show me the stars?"

"All of them."

Leonardo smiled.

The ink bottle sparkled and disappeared.

MOON CHILD

SUSAN STRADIOTTO (300 WORDS)

Honorable Mention

Freed, Réaltín dashed to her love, but Willow stumbled. What evil weakened the strongest faerie she'd known? Willow's smile was thinner, her eyes hollower.

Réaltín caressed her cheek. "What ails you, love?"

A shadow crossed Willow's face, but she demurred. "Nothing to worry over since you've returned to me, my star."

Willow placed a hand over Réaltín's and kissed her with tenderness that narrated her yearning over . . . how many years had passed? Willow tasted sweeter than life, her gentle desperation echoing Réaltín's. They finally held one another again, but what of—

Our baby. Amaris had been so small when the warlock had captured Réaltín. *How could I not have thought of her first?* Réaltín withdrew. "Where's—"

"Amaris?" Willow finished her sentence.

Réaltín's eyes stung. *So long apart, yet still so familiar.* "I-is our moon child grown?"

"No, love. She awaits us at home."

Réaltín sighed her relief, grasping her mate. "Take me to her?"

Willow's breath heaved. "Open the veil. I'll navigate."

Once in Faerie, Willow faltered, fell to her knees. "By *Anu*, he's begun." She latched onto Réaltín, sinking to the forest floor.

"Begun what?"

"Inking a spell, my star."

Searing pain shot through Réaltín's chest; she shoved Willow's sleeve

97

above the elbow. Black tendrils spread from the bend in her arm, crawling toward her heart.

For me? Réaltín wept. "How" —she choked— "could you give that monster blood?"

"He promised"—Willow gasped for breath—"we'd have seventeen days and seventeen nights."

Réaltín wept. "You know better; you cannot trust a warlock."

"To see you again, my star, . . . was worth the price." Willow's body went limp, but her chest rose and fell in shallow measures.

"Don't leave!"

"Our moon child had time with me; now she has you. Give Amaris my love."

NOT ALONE

MINERVA CERRIDWEN (293 WORDS)

A large, black tentacle rose from the page of the ancient tome, and then another, and another—while the letters around them were still melting together into inky pools, thickening until they too became flesh. The spell had worked, and before long, these tentacles were lifting their body out of the book, its pages no longer discernible, clumped together as ink kept gushing out, both strengthening the demon and dripping off the table.

Olwyn stared up at the huge, gleaming face. Where xe expected its eyes, it simply had two even shinier spots.

"I assume you summoned me for a reason," the liquid voice prompted.

"Yes. Right. About that." Olwyn shook xemself out of xyr marvel. "If you'd be willing, I need you to visit my classmates. They think…" Xe took a deep breath. "They think I'm not real. That it's impossible for me to only sometimes have a gender, and for that gender not to be the same all the time. And they don't listen when I explain it, so… When I read about you, I figured they'd find you more convincing."

"I can be *very* convincing." A brilliant grin appeared, black on black.

"But I don't want you to harm anyone, or to just plant ideas in their minds," Olwyn hastened to add. "I just want them to learn that… I exist." Those last words came out quietly.

"Leave it to me." The demon turned toward the door, sending ink splatters everywhere.

"One more thing." The ritual's guidelines had not included this small piece of information, and Olwyn could not suppress xyr curiosity. "If you don't mind telling me… What is your name?"

The tentacles squirmed around with mirth. "I," the creature declared, "am Representation. But *you* can call me Story."

HEART BOUND IN INK
KIM KATIL (293 WORDS)

Honorable Mention

Aria approached the split-rail fence that divided her father's realm from that of the elusive Shadow Fae. She hesitated, but she was not a child to be ruled by nightmare tales, and the crunch of her boots on the deeply packed snow was a reminder of the frost mage that threatened them all.

She gritted her teeth and strode through the gate. Only a mile or so later, the ground rumbled with the hooves of approaching riders. Her breath caught at the sight of the woman who dismounted to face her. The rest of the troop remained in the saddle.

"You trespass." Strikingly beautiful, the woman rested her hand on her sword with an air of lethal control. Her purple eyes were accentuated by purple black hair, and her lithe, tall form was sheathed in dark armor.

"I am Aria, daughter of King Atheon of the Borderlands with a message for the Guardian of the Shadows." Youngest and entirely expendable daughter, but still.

"And I am Silver, Champion of the one you seek. What is your message?" She reached out for the paper clutched in Aria's grasp.

Power slammed through Aria when Silver's hand met her own. She gasped as elaborate vines of darkest green manifested on her hands and then spiraled up her arm. Luminous flowers burst to life in a ripple of purple ink over the vines. Delicate blue blossoms that matched Aria's own eyes traced along the vines that snaked up Silver's arm and made a circlet around her neck.

"Hearts' bound," Silver whispered reverently, echoing the words that filled Aria's soul.

A man's joyous laughter cut through the silence that surrounded them. "Champion, it would see seem we have a mage to defeat and a royal wedding to plan."

CONFESSIONS OF AN INKAHOLIC

J. P. EGRY (288 WORDS)

As a toddler I drew.

I drew on white walls behind my parents' furniture—crude crayon outlines of animals, flowers, cars, and stick people without flesh or genitals.

In school, I progressed to pencil, filling in line figures with muscle and hair and sometimes clothing but still no genitalia.

Obsession with ink renderings overtook me in high school and college. I needed no drug. The ebony flow from my pen brought me a high I'd never felt before. Lacking interest in the opposite sex, or even my own sex, gave me time to extend emotion into art.

I've received continual praise for my detailed, intricate process contrasting black ink and white paper. Yet no one else sees how the drawings come alive and step off the page to greet me.

I work night and day. I rarely take time to eat or drink. I breathe deeply, inhaling the inky aroma filling the air. It is the closest thing to intoxication I know. Multiple sketch pads pile up on the table beside my bed; artist's pens stand in empty peanut butter jars. I fall asleep with nibs uncovered, blobs and scribbly stains appearing on my white sheets.

People ask why I don't date. They don't understand. I have no interest in sex. Some call me "Ace." I find my joy in the fluidity, yet permanence of ink. My creations are my companions. That's all I need.

I tried broader pen points on large canvases. But it wasn't enough. Now I've painted all my walls white—blank pages waiting for my inspiration.

∽

Sorry, I must go now. The figures I created in the dining room have stepped out of the sheetrock and are waiting for dinner at the table.

SCIENCE FICTION PART TWO

"Our problem right now is that we're so specialized that if the lights go out, there are a huge number of people who are not going to know what to do. But within every dystopia there's a little utopia."

— MARGARET ATWOOD

PRINTED LOVE
ROBIN REED (300 WORDS)

Honorable Mention

I loved her.

Her stories, more than a hundred years old, spoke to a lonely, confused little girl. Her depth, her wisdom, her passion.

No one knew that my life's work was dedicated to her. Medical and engineering degrees bent toward one goal. Taking the common, everyday bioprinter to its ultimate end.

She took form in the machine. She was built, molecule by molecule, using the bio ink that I invented.

At the end of each day, running a lab that invented and marketed uses for my discoveries, I retired to the chamber where she was being made.

The entire process took over a month. I stayed with her as much as I could. Sometimes I slept in her chamber. The whirring of the machine soothed me.

Her DNA was found on some her things. It was infused into each cell. When her brain was done the computer put all we knew about her into it. All her own writing and everything written about her. There were gaps. We knew nothing about her grade school or where she lived when she published her first story.

She had one love. A married woman who worked with her. They couldn't be together, they would have been fired, ostracized. But her stories hinted at the life she wanted.

I would tell her how things have changed. How she could be free. With me.

When the machine stopped, she lay, perfect, on the slab. After a few moments, she opened her eyes.

"Hello."

"Nora?" she whispered.

"I am..."

"Nora, I was with you. Where are you?"

History didn't record the name of her love. How did my construction of her know?

She looked through me.

"I want to go back."

The body I had built became empty. She was gone.

I was alone again.

INK IS MEMORY

A.R. MOLER (290 WORDS)

"Do you want her full name?" Daphne looked at Reagan. They'd been married for six years before reaching the decision to have a child.

"I don't know."

"Type it in both ways so that the font will show you what it looks like." Reagan nodded, and tapped the keystrokes into the system that displayed what the tattoo would look like.

Daphne rubbed her hand on Reagan's back. She felt the grief of loss too, but maybe not in quite the same way Reagan did. Regan had been the one carrying the baby. If they had wanted a male child, they would have had to pick a sperm donor, but they had decided on a girl. Thank deities tech had evolved enough that they could use Reagan's egg and extract an appropriate set of chromosomes from one Daphne's to fertilize it. It was their biological child. For nearly nine months everything had gone exactly according to plan, and they had dreamed of holding their daughter in their arms.

And then it had gone horribly wrong. She had almost lost Reagan too. Reagan had been on a shuttle, flying home from Gepa IV, finishing one last business trip before her due date. The landing at the spaceport hadn't been a landing, it had been a crash. Reagan had been badly injured. Their unborn daughter hadn't survived. That was five months ago. Only in the past couple of weeks had Reagan begun to resume something approximating her normal life. They were both trying to move forward.

"Lydia Elle, just the two I think," Reagan murmured.

"Okay. I love you. And I would have loved her too." Daphne traced a fingertip along the upper curve of Regan's breast where the tattoo would be placed.

BALLPOINT

GWEN COHOLAN (276 WORDS)

I see a dot I recognize as Earth. No matter how small it gets, it will never be as cramped as this commuter ship. Security won't let you take anything that isn't considered an absolute necessity. I managed to sneak one thing in, though. I click it twice.

I take the ballpoint pen out of my pocket. It was a gift from someone too beautiful for this world—for any other world too, considering they didn't meet the qualifications for interstellar commute. When I knew them, they were teaching history, their talent only rivaled by their passion for the subject. They stared me down from the other side of their desk one day.

According to them, I was prettier than all the men they knew combined, and they assured me they knew several.

I told them that they were full of shit.

They smiled and handed me this pen. I click it a couple more times.

It was an antique, they said. I knew as much. Writing utensils are obsolete, and have been for nearly a century.

I told them I had no idea.

They smiled again.

I want to write them a letter. Handwritten, but I didn't bring any paper. I should have had the foresight. The irony of a pen without paper would be enough to make them laugh. I picture them doing so and smile.

I still see the dot I recognize as Earth, where we once stood together. It hardly looks big enough for the both of us now. I click the pen once more and point it toward the empty space between us.

I miss you.

I hope it reaches them.

THE AERIUM

JEN RIVERS (299 WORDS)

Honorable Mention

I lay outside our home, staring upwards and dreaming of the sky. The weather is what Jess likes to call 'murky'; one of our captors has blackened the region between our dome and the next. They're hiding something.

"I hope the neighbours are okay." Jess says as she lies down beside me and squeezes my hand. I smile at her use of 'neighbours'. She enjoys naming our new reality to shadow the old.

"Milla?" Her voice cracks and she looks past me, eyes wide. I roll over and am confronted by an array of eyes and limbs watching us from just beyond our dome's skin.

"It's okay. They're just kids." I whisper, but my breathing quickens anyway. We lay motionless, as boring as possible to dissuade our audience. I doubt my plan as a childhood memory surfaces: a fascinating stationary starfish at an aquarium. The squid swim away and a glance confirms we're alone.

I kiss Jess, searching for distraction. I feel her smile against my lips before she pulls away. "Science first." I nod and follow her to the dome's edge. Physicists even now, this unfruitful investigation is our daily ritual. The frictionless skin deforms at my touch. In the back of my mind, I know this technology is beyond us. Beyond all humanity. We keep probing though, unable and unwilling to accept that we're not even prisoners. We're animals in a cage.

The water starts to clear. "The neighbours are gone." Jess says.

"Maybe they escaped," my voice optimistic despite knowing it's unlikely. We're almost 2km under the ocean; even if we could get through the impenetrable barrier, the water would kill us.

"Maybe they escaped." Jess says, her tone sombre. I nod. I return to examining the skin, determined that our freedom will be different.

BLOOD
RJ SCOTT (300 WORDS)

"We've got a live one, Julian. Get down here!"

I crutched down the steps as fast as I could, then stopped in shock as the stench of burning hit me. In its decaying form, this was one of *them* inside the city cordon, acid seeping from each of the lines drawn onto their skin.

"Jesus, fuck, tell me someone is filming this?"

"No, Julian, we're sitting here with our thumbs up our asses," Brody, the lead forensic scientist, glared at me.

I ignored the sarcasm and stared at the unfolding drama of a corpse self-destructing. Was this how it was going to end for me? I pulled at my sleeves, attempting to cover the curving tattoos that were steadily covering my torso and twisting around my fingers as the same acid burned me from inside.

Black as ink, the fluid leaked from the corpse into the ground, scoring marks that mirrored what we'd once thought were just tattoos on flesh— long, twisting designs no one had been able to decipher.

"Brody, fuck," I warned.

He glanced at me and shook his head in caution. *Stay professional.* He was too close. I wanted to drag him out of the way before the acid could reach him. No sense in us both dying.

"There's nothing fucking left to test," he shouted and startled the filming technician so much she yelped, but he wasn't paying attention to her or the liquid splashing near his pants.

"Don't let it touch you."

Please don't make the same mistakes as me.

We fought like cat and dog, in and out of bed, but he would get too close. He would sacrifice his life to find a way to save me.

Even though we both knew it was too late for me. Too late for us all.

LOVE IS BLIND

SHEILA FINCH (294 WORDS)

"Dad!" Thirteen-year-old Megan erupted into Mike's office, dropping her backpack. "Can I invite a new friend to dinner tomorrow?"

Mike looked at the schoolbooks on the floor. "Don't leave your stuff there."

"Okay! But say yes, pretty please?"

"Ask Tony. He's in charge of the kitchen."

"The dad's a scientist at the aquarium, and he doesn't have any friends yet."

"How'd you know about the father's friends?"

"Not the father! I want to invite Jeremy. I think I'm in love."

"You're too young to be going out with boys!"

Megan's hug knocked his glasses sideways. "Not going out, Dad. We'd be here."

In the kitchen, Tony was grating Parmigiana. Mushrooms simmered on the stove; the aroma of garlic filled the air.

"Pops. Can my new boyfriend come to dinner tomorrow?"

Tony put the cheese down. "Aren't you a bit young for a boyfriend?"

"You two are SO old-fashioned!" Megan pouted. "Jeremy's different. I think he might've been adopted, like me."

Tony sighed. "Will he be okay with –"

"Of course! He likes everything."

"Not what I meant, Meggie."

But she'd already bounced out.

~

FRIDAY, Tony went shopping early, and Mike put his work aside to vacuum the house. The dining table was set. Good smells from the kitchen, something Italian. Megan and her new friend arrived.

Not a jock, Mike thought, but such thick glasses!

Skinny kid needs to eat better, Tony decided. And who wears long-sleeve shirts anymore?

They took their seats. Megan did most of the talking. "Great salad, Pops! What's next?"

Tony brought the steaming bowl. "Linguine with calamari in ink sauce."

The kid jumped up, screaming, arms waving in air.

Megan shrieked. "I told you Jeremy's different!"

Not arms, Tony saw. Tentacles.

Oh well, Mike thought. *Never did like squid anyway.*

MEET CUTE
ADRIK KEMP (299 WORDS)

Whistling, screaming cacophonous explosions reverberated through the reinforced steel of the protected smartink weapons tank. Within, the weapons artist Pia wielded a tattoo needle, applying designs with deft precision to sheets of metal, paper and skin. Soldiers streamed in and out through protected entrances on the floor, eager for new tools to combat the enemy.

A tall, buff, bronzed woman laid down her tessellating gun, undid the latches on her sleeve and exposed her forearm for Pia. She tensed and her musculature danced under her skin.

"Gimme something long range, clean, hard to detect," she winked at Pia. "I heard you're one of the best, don't let me down."

Pia gulped but only hesitated a moment before beginning. The soldier gritted her teeth but bore the pain well as Pia injected smartink – a combination of classic ink, nano-electric particles and femtoAI – into the upper layer of the soldier's skin. Pia sketched power sources, insulation, acceleration and drift tubes plus expanding architecture and fuel from the soldier's wrist, around her forearm and up almost to her shoulder. She was efficient and before long, she nodded her consent for the soldier to rise.

"Ready, aim, fire?" the soldier asked.

Pia nodded, held out her arm for the soldier to mimic and gave her the code to activate. As she did, the smartink glowed and transformed. Parts solidified above the soldier's skin, held in place by magnetic fields. Energy crackled from her elbow to her palm. The soldier uncocked her arm and ripped off her sleeve for access. She leaned over to Pia, winked again and kissed her on the cheek. "Thanks babe. When we're done, I'll owe you a drink."

And then she was gone, leaving Pia stunned, blush blooming on her cheeks and her tattoo needle limp in her hand.

BLANK AS THE PAGE
STEVE FUSON (300 WORDS)

The other kids have no trouble writing their biographies. Some of them never run out of ideas. But when I think about my future, my mind is as blank as the page.

My mother reminds me that it's a privilege to write my own future. The lower castes have little say in how their lives unfold. Some people aren't fit to write their own story, she says.

I worry that might include me.

"Start with something easy," she says. "Pick your gender. What feels right?"

"I don't know."

"How about a career? What do you enjoy doing?"

"I don't know."

The help have lots of suggestions, mostly involving creative genitalia or not having to take orders. And when they don't know I'm listening, they have some nasty ideas for the elite.

Everybody has something they want. What's wrong with me, that I don't?

I think about running away, but where would I go? The elite are well documented. I couldn't pretend to be someone else's child. And only the elite are born with potential. I wouldn't be able to hide among the lower castes' gendered children.

I work up the nerve to ask, "What happens to kids who don't write their biography?"

"Someone helps them. Their parents or other students. Letting someone else write your own future defeats the purpose, but if you haven't written your biography when you turn 13, you die."

So I sit, afraid to touch pen to paper, knowing I need to write something, knowing anything I write will be permanent. Nothing feels right. I see the elite and I see the lower castes and I don't want any part of it. At a loss, I scribble on every page, covering them until they're black. Then I close the book and wait to see what happens.

DRAGON BLOOD
BENOIT LAFORTUNE (290 WORDS)

The Silver Dragon mark means I lead a group of chosen warriors to defend Terra-Clusters. When we transform, the Aegis makes sure we speak the same language, no matter our species. When I'm here, piloting the Dragonborn, fighting Kaiju, I'm free.

However, I know life's about to change forever. Tonight, I'm having dinner with my father, five long years after I sent him the letter.

"Kimbo, go for the left flank, I'll charge it dead center!" I shout as I start running, summoning Silverclaw, my magical mecha-sword.

Fearing my dad is ridiculous. Here I am, in a giant Samurai robot fighting a space demon but I'm terrified of a 5'7 accountant. Here I fought, right in the thick of it, and all I could think about was the damn letter.

Oxblood ink was a proper base, of course, as red signifies love, pain, and passion… it gave life to the letter, but it wasn't enough. It needed to shine, to express inner light. I progressively added pure silver to it. It made the ink complete, as if it were healing, changing, becoming what it was meant to be all along. Just like my own, its journey was necessary. With a dash of silver, the oxblood had revealed to the world how glorious Dragon Blood ink could be.

"Anya, fire breath now!"

Kimbo and I got out of the way just in time. The flames engulfing the Kaiju were exactly like my anxiety, all-consuming and spectacular.

We teleported back to the base to celebrate another victory, but my mind races at the thought of tonight. For the first time in years, I would be seeing my father; he would finally meet the badass woman his little boy turned out to be.

BUTTERFLY

GEORGIA COOK (300 WORDS)

The tattooist was accustomed to strange requests: drunken teens demanding Martian curse words, nervous lovers inking pet names across their forearms, sailors on shore-leave from vast outer-galaxy cargo ships, bristling with holographic tattoos, offering currency from across the stars.

The tattooist liked the sailors the best; liked their stories as she inked their star-burned skin, though never had she thought to travel in their footsteps. Never even thought to try.

ONE DAY A GIRL entered the shop and handed the tattooist a folded scrap of paper.

"It's called a butterfly," the girl explained. "Do you think you can ink it?" she pointed to a spot on her arm. "Right here."

The tattooist had seen Earth-animals before, in holograms meticulously constructed from ancient bones: birds and insects, seals and cats; all as strange as anything from that doomed grey planet. But never a photograph. Never something so tactile.

It was beautiful.

This close, the girl smelt of vanilla and Venus suntraps. The tattooist's hands had never felt so clumsy, her fingers so inept.

"Why a butterfly?" she asked, as she readied her pen.

The girl blushed. "It's a dead thing," she said. "A vanished thing from a forgotten world. But I can carry it with me now, whenever I go. Do you understand?"

The Tattooist felt she had never understood anything so clearly in her life. Never been so jealous of a vanished thing. And she kissed the girl, again and again and again.

ONCE THE GIRL WAS GONE, the tattooist took the photograph from her pocket and stared at it in the darkness.

Out there was an ink-and-flesh duplicate-- a butterfly ghost, carried on the arm of a girl who smelt of vanilla and flowers-- dancing among the stars.

And the smallest piece of the tattooist, dancing along with it.

TOBY'S TATTOO

JAMIE SANDS (299 WORDS)

"It's a memorial, of sorts."

"Sorry for your loss," the tattooist said in a detached way, already distracted.

He was getting the tattoo to mourn, that much was true. He'd lost his best friend.

More than that, the love of his life.

Micah.

His fingers long and slender, playing a love song for Toby on the antique piano.

She finished drawing on Toby's arm, started sterilising needles.

"It's alright," Toby said. "It's better this way."

She nodded, although Toby thought he sounded like he was rejoicing the death of a friend, of true love.

Not that Micah was dead.

The last Toby had heard he was a guest at some music festival on the huge ship where the Bahamas had been, before the oceans rose. It had been all over social media. The golden child, Micah, playing his songs.

The ones he'd written for Toby. Or. Maybe some of them had been written for the previous Toby. Or the one before that… impossible to know.

The tattooist started to work. Toby's jaw clenched, he could blame it on the needle, this tension, but really it was the train of thought.

MICAH NEVER TOLD HIM, definitively, how many had come before. Which number iteration Toby was, and in some ways it didn't matter.

He was free now. And this tattoo? It was insurance.

Evidence that whatever Micah, or his bio-fabrication father did, they couldn't erase him. He would always be unique. If they ever tracked him down, or worse, if the next iteration of Toby found him...

Time flew by. His jaw clenched and his teeth ached.

FINALLY, she held up a mirror so Toby could see it, red and raw but beautifully indelible. A bird, flying free of a cage in bright sunshine yellow.

"What do you think?"

"Perfect."

HORROR

"Life and death appeared to me ideal bounds, which I should first break through, and pour a torrent of light into our dark world."

— MARY SHELLEY

THE COLLECTION

ELLIOT COOPER (300 WORDS)

"Ready to add to the collection?" Cassidy asked.

"Yeah." I glanced down at the pine tree tattoo encircling my forearm, then ran a finger over my top surgery scars through my t-shirt. Three years of healing inside and out was enough. I felt ready. "Time to cover these with something cool."

A door stood open at the end of the corridor, soft golden light emanating from within. We entered the small room, its brick walls painted in smears of unexpectedly ugly pus-like colors.

The tattoo artist sat on a stool and smiled. Bald and shirtless, most of his pale skin was decorated and on display.

"Blaine?" I asked.

"And you're Axel. Right on time. Get comfortable and we'll begin." He motioned to the dentist-style chair beside him, then turned to greet Cassidy.

Light bounced off the walls. They glowed as if lit by inner light. I winced, looked away, and lifted my shirt over my head, focusing instead on Blaine's illustrated shoulders.

He and Cassidy hummed a melody. She snapped her fingers and tapped her boot in time. It sounded vaguely familiar—something she'd played in the car. A lilting, droning tune underscored by otherworldly lyrics.

"Um, guys?" I ventured in confusion.

Their voices rose and something unseen pinned me to the chair.

"Hey!"

Rich vocals erupted from Blaine. His back muscles tensed, flexed, *danced*. The yellow glow pulsed with Cassidy's rhythm.

Black tendrils of runes, skulls, and labyrinthine geometry pulsed impossibly off Blaine's skin. The ink lines snaked through the air, surged toward me, grasping, pulling me *in*.

I screamed as light pulsed dark.

My eyes opened to see ancient pines spearing a shimmering golden sky. The cloudless expanse coalesced into a hazy reflection of the mirror on Blaine's wall. He grinned down at my tattoo on his arm.

TEMPORARY/PERMANENT
BROOKE K. BELL (298 WORDS)

Marianne paced the length of the small hall that connected the living room, and the door to the outside, to the bedroom, and the door to the inside. Temporary steps, tracing a path towards a temporary solution to a permanent problem.

Beyond the crack of the door, she saw her wife sleeping soundly in the cool of the late night. Temporary wife, temporary bedroom. She ran a hand down her bare upper arm, over the small black mark vaguely in the shape of a hook, torso braless in a white tank and boxer shorts. Her long legs carried her back to the closet. Pulling on joggers, boots, and a black jacket.

She tousled what was left of her cropped black hair in the bathroom mirror and grabbed her house keys. Exited the dark apartment into the bleak, cold night. She wished she could curl back under the covers with her wife, but this would not fix her permanent chill. *You're always so freezing.* Marianne's laugh at this was both an alarm and a welcoming ring.

The first warm body came in an alleyway, easily drained, black blood like the black ink on her arm, a mark of permanence in a world of constant change. But Marianne didn't change. She simply adapted.

There were always more warm bodies. There was only one of her.

The second body of the night came around a corner, fresh from dancing. Blood chalky from powdered drugs, but suitable enough. Marianne hazily returned back to her small apartment, home of a series of temporary lives, her stomach full, her mind clear. She slipped off her boots and jacket and curled in next to her wife. Another warm body. One she hoped she would not bring harm.

Some things are temporary, and some are permanent.

IMPENDING AFFAIR

R. H. ARGENT (300 WORDS)

She dipped the quill a final time, completed the design, and sat back to admire her handiwork. Not bad for a first attempt. It had taken many delicious hours, more to get the subject just right.

She turned and reached for the tome, pulling it near to mutter the impenetrable words that writhed as she spoke.

The imp, barely a foot tall, blinked into existence a moment later. It gave itself a little shudder and glanced furtively at its surroundings before bringing its gaze upon her and breaking into the broadest smile she'd ever seen.

"Good job, witch," it squeaked.

"Thanks, but I wouldn't go that far. Dabbler perhaps."

"Still, I'm impressed. It's nice someone invited me back," it said, whipping its tail. "Aren't many who'd do such a thorough job. Problem is, no one believes anymore. They make a half-hearted attempt, so of course it doesn't work." It looked down and asked, "Is this the one?"

She shook her head. "That one's mine."

It tittered, displaying a mouth full of pointy teeth. "Did you make a start with the other one as well?"

"No, she's all yours."

The imp's smile widened. "I like you used fresh blood. Matches my complexion," it laughed. "Got the token?"

She passed over the lock of sable hair, from her soon-to-be *very* ex-wife, and said, "Take your time."

"You bet. After being away so long, I'm gonna have me some fun," and with that it vanished.

She regarded the body of the woman, staring back at her wide-eyed. Bitch. She'd made certain the knots were tight, made sure she couldn't wriggle and ruin her calligraphy, etched along her thighs and across her belly and breasts. She picked up the blade she'd used to dig the inkwell out of her navel. Now, where was she?

THE ROSE TATTOO

HELEN M. MERRICK (297 WORDS)

"Anything?"

"Anything. Just say the word."

"Okay." Peaches nodded toward the girl at the next table. "How about that?" She pointed to the girl's arm. "It's beautiful."

"You want a tattoo?"

Peaches grinned.

"Really? Okay... Excuse me," said Jessica, reaching out to tap the girl's shoulder. "Hi. Sorry to disturb you. May I look at your tattoo?"

"Erm—" The girl smiled awkwardly but held out her arm.

"Oh, that's quite something."

"Told you," said Peaches. "Look at the rich colour in the rose petals and the way the stems twist together. And it's exactly the size I want. It's us," she said, taking Jessica's hand in hers. "Two beautiful roses entwined forever."

"Is it unique?" Jessica asked the girl. "Or copied from a catalogue that any—"

"I drew it," said the girl. "I designed all my tattoos."

"Did you?" Jessica held up her phone. "May I?" She photographed the girl's arm and a similar smaller design inked onto her neck. "Pretty," she said. "Thank you."

"Well?" Peaches fluttered long lashes.

"If it's what you want."

"It is."

"Not a holiday? Diamond earrings?"

Peaches giggled. "You know I hate clichés."

"Yes, but I can get you *anything*."

"I know. I want the tattoo. It's symbolic of our love."

Aw, you're so romantic." Jessica kissed her nose. "Okay, I'll make some calls."

Peaches ordered more coffee while Jessica talked into her phone. She smiled at Jessica's serious face and fist-pumped the air when Jess gave the thumbs-up.

"Seriously? That quick?"

Jessica nodded. "They're coming for her now. I've got a surgeon prepared to do the graft tomorrow and I'm er… I'm thinking of having the roses from her neck."

"Yes!" Peaches clapped her hands. "Great idea, matching tattoos."

"Oh, Babe, I love you," said Jessica. "Happy anniversary."

I AM HAPPY TO BE HERE TODAY
ELSA M CARRUTHERS (299 WORDS)

Honorable Mention

"Support group works if you work it. Remember to always remind yourself of how happy you are to be here. Tomorrow is never promised." That little nugget of wisdom from Michael, the oldest Transperson Layla'd ever met.

55 years old. Young really, and yet she couldn't keep from thinking of him with reverence. Wise and long-lived. She lovingly thought of him as her Yoda.

She'd cry about that, and all the lives cut short if she wasn't already spent. Goddamn it, she couldn't deal with the loss of Katrina. And she couldn't get past the senseless brutality of Katrina's last moments. It made her want to do ugly things. Mean and evil things. Replace the beauty they killed with something hideous. It was what those monsters deserved.

"I am happy to be here today," Layla said the group mantra to herself. And she was. She was grateful for her life, even if Katrina was gone. But her sense of peace and safety were gone. And her work was suffering. Instead of the cute and brightly colored panels she was supposed to draw for a graphic novel called Art-emis, she found herself drawing dark, brooding land and seascapes. Churning waves that tore apart Katrina's attackers. She drew and inked their faces with particular care, freezing their last moments of agony in each frame.

And when she heard that one somehow drowned in his pretrial cell, she knew it was her doing. She concentrated on drawing the other two. One mowed down by a car in the desert, still alive as the vultures picked him apart; her pen elongating the vulture's claws.

The last one, the worst, she'd think of something particularly gruesome for him. Layla smiled and started sketching.

"I am happy to be here today," she said to herself.

BLIND DATE

RAINIE ZENITH (299 WORDS)

Carmel sipped her cappuccino and pondered whether to tell Rochelle she hunted vampires.

Rochelle was petite, with long charcoal hair and a perfect ski jump nose. A small star tattoo adorned her right cheek. She was beyond cute. The blind date to end all dates, blind or otherwise.

Would she still be interested if she knew about the hunting?

Carmel fretted. She didn't want to scare Rochelle off, but hunting was her life's work; not something she could keep secret for long.

"This might sound a bit weird," she said, setting down her mug. She glanced around. The cafe was empty this late in the day. No-one to overhear.

She inhaled.

"I hunt vampires."

Rochelle's eyes widened.

"No way! There's only a handful of vampire hunters left in the world. I should know; I'm one of them! Honestly Carmel, what are the chances?"

The odds were so unlikely that Carmel put Rochelle to the test.

"How to identify one?"

"Lack of a shadow. Bat tattoo on back of neck. The fangs, of course."

"How to kill one?"

"Lop off the head with a sword of silver. It's the only way."

"How to avoid becoming one?"

"Don't get close enough for them to bite you!"

Yes, Rochelle was the real deal.

She pointed at Carmel's left hand.

"What's your tattoo represent?"

Carmel glanced down at her skull and crossbones.

"Death. I bring death to vampires. What about yours?"

Carmel gently stroked the little star on Rochelle's cheek.

"It means I'm a superstar of my craft."

Carmel leaned closer, eyes focused on Rochelle's lips.

"The craft of hunting vampires or of making love?"

She nuzzled beneath Rochelle's hair, discovering a bat tattoo on the woman's neck.

Uh-oh.

"The craft of converting hunters to the dark side," Rochelle grinned, revealing her fangs.

A FLACON OF INK

DEAN WELLS (300 WORDS)

Jamie staggers towards me, the floorboards under his feet slick with lique-fied flesh. Unspeakable guilt compels me to watch as my handiwork slides across what remains of his person, trails of malicious ink coursing around the hairs on his chest, his arms, his legs. Tribal patterns, shifting before my eyes.

My dear Jamie, desecrated where the ink has chewed and devoured and dissolved. Death should have taken him, as it had for so many. God help me, I'd prayed for that mercy, not this slow festering decay. His arm reaches out as he lurches closer, his fingers grasping, the other arm gone. The hunger is upon him now, his erection declaring a desire so foreign to my own--the mindless yearning to consume, to replenish the flesh that the ink has melted away.

I cannot say where the ink originated, the curious bottle was simply there amid the pens and irons and pigments of my craft; its contents calling to me, wanting to be used. And make use of it I did--on Jamie, on the fellows we'd secreted into our bed, on the neighborhood men who quietly visited my shop. The flacon never emptied. It was always full.

The inked swarm outside my door now, quiet no more; clawing, wheez-ing, my name decried by those who can still speak, cursing me for inflicting this terror upon them. All they'd wanted was to express their individuality, to acknowledge themselves, to simply be seen.

One bullet remains in a firearm that was only meant for show. I'd reserved that bullet for me. Instead--and in the presence of that cursed flacon of ink--I force myself to aim, and I end Jamie's suffering square between his empty, beautiful eyes.

My shop door crashes open, and the inked surge inside to feed.

SQUID ON THE BEACH
CLAIRE DAVON (295 WORDS)

The squid flopped on the sand, spewing black ink as it contorted. A dozen such creatures dotted the vista, their arms contracting and expanding as their life essence ebbed. I picked up the nearest one, its slimy skin slick in my hand, and managed to toss it into the waves.

"Gross," Joanie said. She stepped on the next one, grinding her heel into it before lifting it off and wiping it on the damp sand.

I knew what they had once been. I'd dreamed of the primal ancient gods at night, those who only surfaced when the world was dark. They'd told me what they were going to do and spared me the same fate. She might not be so quick to destroy the beast if she was aware of what it actually was. Or maybe that was a fantasy, driven by the fading remains of a potential future for us.

"I only kiss girls when I'm drunk, hon. It meant nothing."

I'd seen the cruelty in her before, the casual disregard of other's feelings. The dismissal of mine.

Now the old gods had too. Maybe I'd brought her here for that reason. I would never be sure.

Joanie lifted her foot to step on another squid, her face distorting with malice. I calculated whether I could slide the animal out from under her marauding heel before it came down. The ocean roared with fury, the waves swelling…and there was one more squid on the sand. It opened its mouth in horror as it writhed in the air that had been its life's blood moments earlier.

I debated before getting a grip on the squirming creature and flinging it into the water. I heard her shouting my name as she sank.

Or maybe I didn't.

141

FANTASY PART THREE

"As great scientists have said and as all children know, it is above all by the imagination that we achieve perception, and compassion, and hope."

— URSULA K. LE GUIN

FAITH AND THE THORNCUTTERS

DIE BOOTH (294 WORDS)

"They're only insects. They don't feel a thing."

Derora doubted that. When they were tipped into the boiling water, the Thorncutters screamed. "How can you know that?"

Sister Cecilia smiled, mildly. "Think of it this way. They're fulfilling their destiny. Giving their lives to spread the Wisdom. Just like you are, my dear."

Derora knew about giving things up for others, but wasn't convinced the thick, wine-coloured ink was worth dying for, no matter how wonderful the illumination it produced. It was used to beautify. Not just manuscript pages, but the lips and cheeks of the wealthy. She'd never used it, not even before the Sanctum, back when she'd worn the appearance of a high society gentleman. She looked into the seething mass of beetles in their vast copper cauldron. They emanated a chirruping whirr that sounded almost meditative. "I'm not sure they can read."

Sister Cecilia gave a short, sad laugh. "Oh, Derora, you just have to have faith."

∾

FAITH. It was kind of her purpose now. The Wisdom told you to live your truth, but people told you what your truth was. They captured the Wisdom,

145

trapped it on pages. She stared at the ceiling above her bunk. Maybe the ink would have more to tell us if it stayed inside the Thorncutters.

Quietly, she rose. Pulled on clothes and packed a satchel. Carried her shoes, feet light along corridors she knew by heart.

The cauldron lid crashed like a tolling bell as she heaved it to the floor. In the starlight the beetles' bodies flashed garnet, rising up in a cloud around her as she laughed in delight. Their wings brushed her face, gentle, glittering, as she ran with them out into the night, taking flight in glorious true colour.

THE STORIES that impressed me the most were those that managed to use the sparse 300-word limit to offer a glimpse into a fully-developed speculative world. Only a few stories achieved this monumental feat, and "Faith and the Thorncutters" was without a doubt one of the most successful in that regard. This story truly makes every single word count, resulting in a rich narrative that feels so much more expansive than any 294 little words have any right to be. An all around excellent story that showcases just how much a skilled author can accomplish with only a few words!

—Devon Widmer

POWER

K. ATEN (298 WORDS)

A bell hanging from the door of Karmic Skin jingled as a tall, bearded man with a shaved head pushed inside. He wore a collection of white supremacy tats up and down his arms, and the name tag on his dirty, blue work shirt read "Charles."

He stared at Parker, focused on the undercut black hair and moon phases tattoo circling their neck like a choker. "You some sort of fag, or just a dyke?"

Parker shrugged. "Dyke, but whatever works for you man, I'm just here to do the ink."

"Sign on the door says you'll do anything."

"That's right." Parker stood, knowing the man was going to stay to get tatted.

Charles jabbed a thumb to his left. "Pansies down the street won't ink anything with power, if you know what I mean."

"Yes, sir." Parker gestured toward the sign on the wall. "Rates are there and based on size, cash up front. All the art in here is mine."

A big, leather wallet came out and money was exchanged. "Six-inch skull and crossbones on my back, with the SS carved into the forehead."

Parker took the cash, then sketched a sample. "Something like this?"

"Yeah, that's perfect."

Hours later, Charles finished buttoning his shirt and strode from the room toward the front door. He looked over his shoulder before leaving to see Parker staring at him. "Your shit's cheap but good. I'll send my friends your way, don't even matter if you're a fucking queer or whatever."

Parker smiled, "Please do." Charles left and Parker went back into the tattoo room to cap the special ink they used when consequences were due. A little magically-spelled nightshade went a long way. It wouldn't be the power Charles was looking for, but it was what he deserved.

INKSTICKS AND PAPER SWANS

JAMIE LACKEY (300 WORDS)

The round stone room that they lock the poet in contains nothing but a writing desk.

The desk, of course, is fully stocked. Piles of creamy paper, elegantly carved sable-fur brushes, a pyramid of neatly stacked inksticks, and an inkstone, its well full of perfectly still water.

Sunlight streams down from a single window, high overhead and barred. Too high to reach even when she stands on the desk, its thin legs wobbling beneath her.

There is no escape. Only the tools of her trade.

Her enemies think they've won. That they can keep her caged but still enjoy her song, like a nightingale. They think that her princess will forget her, now that the tempting catalyst of her presence is removed.

The poet picks up the brush that they so kindly provided, and she writes.

Every brushstroke is a love letter, a call to action, a rebellion.

Her enemies don't see the power in her poems. They don't feel the words peel off of the page and etch themselves into readers' hearts--perhaps because their hearts are dried husks in their chests.

They do not understand the discontent that spreads. They have the princess in hand. The poet is locked in her tower, producing verses about flowers and sunlight and swift-flying birds.

They stop publishing her poems, so she folds them into paper swans and releases them to fly up and out through her barred window.

She writes till she runs out of paper, then she turns her brush to the stone walls, the floor, her own skin. The ink is smooth and cool, and she wonders if she can fold herself into a swan to fly away.

Then the door opens, and her princess is there, clutching a bloody sword, and she can finally put down her brush.

BELONGING
DALE PARNELL (299 WORDS)

Even in the dark of the club, she stood out. She approached me slowly, hypnotically, laying a hand on my arm as she leaned in close enough for me to feel her warm breath on my neck.

"I want to buy you a drink," she said, her voice like silk.

She attracted the attention of the young barman with ease and ordered two shots of a honey-coloured liqueur.

"Your tattoos are amazing," I blurted. I had been out almost a year, but still found flirting difficult.

She smiled, downing her drink in one smooth movement. I followed suite, feeling her eyes on me. Taking my hand, we wordlessly sneaked out of the club, following abandoned, dimly lit streets to her flat.

As she slipped out of her clothes, I marvelled at the extent of her tattoos, each one hugging the contours of the next, leaving almost no naked skin. Most depicted animals, with exotic vines woven amongst them, and when she moved, the leaves seemed to tremble in a soft breeze.

"What are you?" she purred, coming closer to me.

"What do you mean?" I stuttered. "I'm... a lesbian."

She laughed warmly, taking my hands in hers and kissing me for the first time, her lips so soft, her skin so warm. She stepped backwards, holding her arms out to her side, and looking down she indicated the sweeping artwork on her body.

"What are you?" she repeated.

"An eagle," I whispered.

She smiled again, eying me hungrily as I removed my clothes, and we embraced suddenly, the heat of her touch burning me, consuming me.

In the morning she dressed, choosing to wear my old jacket rather than her own, as on her chest the fresh ink of a soaring eagle settled amongst its neighbours.

I was hers.

THE SUMMONING

W. DALE JORDAN (297 WORDS)

Honorable Mention

"Handsome and strong," he wrote in enchanted red ink on fresh parchment.

"A smile like sunshine," he continued in orange.

"Creative and kind." The yellow ink made him smile.

"A steward of nature," he wrote in green.

"And loyal," he lettered in blue.

"Wise and discerning," he wrote finally, the purple ink soaking into the paper.

He smiled.

Perhaps, this time, he had gotten it right.

The young magician moved to the fire, casting herbs over the flames, and intoning the spells his Master taught him. Surely, this time, a man he could love and hold dear to his heart would appear.

He felt magic grow around him as the flames grew higher and smiled. This was his favorite part. No matter the outcome, this feeling drew him back to magic every single time.

He carefully dropped the parchment into the flames and fell back as sparks flew into the sky. This was different. The last seven times, this had not happened. He held his breath as a shadow appeared just beyond fire. He shielded his eyes, trying to see who had entered his circle.

A soft *ruff* caught his ears, and he frowned, as an adorable collie pranced close to the fire.

"*Not* what I was going for," he muttered. "Why isn't this spell working?"

"Magnus! Magnus, where are you?"

The magician looked up as a handsome man stumbled into the clearing, a leash in his hand. He was tall, strong, handsome.

"Oh, hi," the newcomer said, smiling warmly. "I'm Jameson. Sorry. Magnus didn't disturb you, did he?"

"Not at all. I'm Alex. Care to join me?"

Trust the words; write your intentions. Sometimes, the magic works in ways you can't expect.

His teacher's words echoed in his ears as Jameson grinned and moved in closer.

MENDING
BLAINE D. ARDEN (297 WORDS)

"Words have power," Pop said when he first taught me how to make my own inks. "But without the right colour and shade, words are nothing but a collection of random letters that fall apart in the slightest breeze."

The warmth of his hands on my shoulders lingered in my mind as I dipped a strip of handmade paper into the slow-boiling creel leaves. Waiting for the ink to dry and show its true colour, I studied the bright orange aura of the damaged statue, ignoring the scattered reds around the fracture. Had I let the leaves simmer long enough?

The ink dried into a decent orange, though not a perfect match. I strained a bit of the liquid into a small vial. Taking deep breaths to centre myself, I dipped a brush into the orange ink. After another deep breath, I released my energy, letting it flow into the statue as I wrote one single word across the fracture: *mend*.

Pop had favoured *restore*.

The dye dripped uselessly down the statue onto the table.

With a snap of my fingers, I relit the fire, tapping my foot as I let the creel leaves simmer again. Test after test, the colour brightened until I didn't dare push it any further. Too far meant starting again tomorrow.

This time the word, the ink, held and sank deep into the statue as I fed it more energy.

Grabbing a reed pen, I allowed myself a small smile at my success while I hiked up my tunic. Tiny scars, some old, some new, all spelling the same word, decorated my ribs just below the wrappings binding my chest.

My breath hitched as the ink dribbled unaffected down my side.

One day I *would* find the right colour to mend me.

ROUGAROUS INC

LAURA J. KELLY (298 WORDS)

Jacob, my partner, was a rougarou until I changed him back to human. It meant trading places, because love sometimes involves sacrifice. Now I'm the first employee in his new business that pairs rougarous with cops, Rougarous Incorporated. Jacob is riding along on our first case. Here I am, the ink barely dry on the contract, proving rougarous have a place in society, and my partner is watching. Nope, no pressure at all.

"Ric, start with those crates," the cop said, pointing to the corner.

I walk around each one sniffing for Eau de drugs. Halfway down the aisle, I stop next to a crate labeled printer/copier ink and nod my doggie head up and down. The cop begins shifting boxes. The top layer is clean. I'm nervous. What if I'm wrong? I look over at Jacob, and he winks. "You got this," he whispers just loud enough for my dog ears.

I signal the third layer reeks with the shit. The cop takes out her kit, opens a random box, and pulls out a bottle filled with black dust. She does her thing, grinning triumphantly when the sample tests positive. "Good job, Ric." She places the bottle on the stack of boxes and calls the processing team as she walks to the entrance with her police tape.

My doggie smile is fierce with pride until I bump against the boxes. The bottle falls, and a cloud of dust rises. So, this is what it's like getting high.

The cops should have realized it was possible. We didn't think to ask if dogs could get high. Not that rougarous would necessarily react the same way. We're only half-dog, after all. You can bet we're going to ink a hazardous duty clause into the contract before the next case.

SPIDER LEGS

E. F. SCHRAEDER (300 WORDS)

Honorable Mention

Ellis shook her head. "The blue one? Since I was twelve. Practically as far back as my memories go."

Jade slid a finger on Ellis' forearm. "And the purple spider?" Jade ignored the crowd at the park, inching closer on the swing.

Ellis tensed.

"We're two people on a park bench. No one will notice." The seat creaked while Jade rocked. "Let's break this down. You can be honest or push me away. Your call."

Ellis whistled. "Dang. That's direct." She rubbed her chin, then nodded. "Okay. Some time after my first lover. We made promises. She didn't keep them. Then the ink changed color."

"I'm sorry." Jade stroked Ellis' arm. "It's still beautiful."

Ellis didn't comment.

"Do you remember what it looked like before?"

"Nope. Memories fade as the color changes, as promised."

Jade arched a dark eyebrow. "Should I be jealous? I mean, do you still think of her?"

Ellis covered her face with her hands, laughing. "Well, you can't hurt if you don't remember. That's the whole point of getting memory inked, isn't it?"

Jade set a hand on Ellis' leg. "I never met anyone who did it that young. I wondered if it really worked."

"I hear that. At first, I thought of her, just a few vague things like where we met. Nothing beyond the barest impressions. Once the purple spread from the legs to the web, I remembered even less. No emotion, just basic facts."

"Is she just a blank spot to you?"

"No, it's not amnesia. She's just imprecise, like a shadow."

Jade's expression tightened. "Do you ever regret it?"

"Never. Why would I want to hurt?"

Jade tilted her face toward Ellis. "And what about second chances? Does the ink make room for that?" As their lips touched, violet faded to lavender.

PANGRAM

SHERYL R. HAYES (298 WORDS)

"Woman!" the feminine voiced boomed. "I am here to pass judgment."

I leapt from my desk. Onyx eyes set an a smoked-crystal feminine face stared at me from where the flatscreen TV should have been. "Judgment?" I squeaked.

She arched an eyebrow. "You summoned me to judge your cow." The head shrunk to a somewhat human size. That was the only thing human about her. A scorpion's tail curved over a lion's body framed with eagles' wings. "Really, you summoned me for such a trivial task?"

I stared at the sphinx. "I thought your kind was more into riddles."

Her wings ruffled, gemstone clicking against gemstone. "I take whatever work I can get it since Odysseus and Homer spread around the answer to my best riddle."

"Oh." I glanced at the menu from the Greek restaurant my girlfriend Myra and I had eaten takeout from last night. I'd smeared blood on the stylized logo after accidentally cutting my finger on a pair of scissors. I decided to test a new keyboard. Tired of quick brown foxes, I typed 'Sphinx of black quartz, judge my vow.' I missed hitting 'v,' turning vow into cow as blood oozed onto the keys.

Where was I going to find a cow in the middle of San Francisco? "I can have some burgers delivered."

The sphinx snorted. She narrowed her eyes. "Your arm, woman. Show me your arm."

"My name is Nicole," I snorted. I turned my hand palm up, revealing the tattoo.

She studied the bovine face with sweeping horns that hid my ex-girlfriend's name. "I declare it to be a good cow." And with that, she retracted into the widescreen.

I sat back and sighed, relieved I didn't have to tell her it was actually my zodiac sign, Taurus the bull.

OPENINGS

K.L. NOONE (300 WORDS)

"It's an opening-spell." Cyan traced spidery black ink like thorns. "A powerful one. No wonder it's scrambled. No accidental use."

"Can you solve it?"

"Of course. But I don't know that I should." He regarded the librarian who'd brought the scroll; Harrington Burke had short sandy hair and intelligent blue eyes, and had tackled cataloguing the late Duke of Gyre's eclectic hazardous library with cheerful expertise. Cyan, tall and dark and awkward, the youngest professor at the Magicians' Convivium, felt himself grow more clumsy and incoherent each time they met.

Harrington had first sought him out to get a bibliomancer's advice about a troublesome grimoire. Cyan, startled amid book-boxes in his brand-new office, had found himself breathless at sun-hued friendliness, knocking at his door.

He did not know what to say now. Touching letters, he caressed power from a long-ago enchanter's pen. Ink gave ideas body, shape, threads weaving past and present and future; this ink held puzzles. It tempted his magic.

Harrington raised eyebrows. "Dangerous?"

"All words can be. But think about being able to open anything, one time. *Anything.*"

Harrington's expression changed. "Don't solve it, then."

"I won't."

"D'you want it? For the Convivium Library. Magical."

"Oh," Cyan said. "Yes, probably. I'll ask. Thank you."

"Should you keep touching it?"

Dangerous, indeed. He put it down. "Probably not. Thank you again."

Harrington lingered. "There's ink on your thumb."

"Earlier. A copying-spell."

"Ah." Harrington swung away, turned back. "About openings. Taking risks. Here. For you." He dropped a folded page onto Cyan's desk, and vanished.

Cyan, perplexed, unfolded paper. Graceful violet script inquired, *Dinner, with me, tonight?*

Bashful wanting lingered in the writing: a form of asking Harrington'd hoped a bibliomancer might like.

Dinner. Possibilities. An opening. Magic, Cyan thought, feeling himself begin to smile. Given voice in ink.

FOR POSTERITY'S SAKE

NATHANIEL TAFF (299 WORDS)

"Do you have to write tonight?" Miri was exhausted and the constant scratch of her tentmate's quill was making sleep impossible.

Rila dipped her quill into her inkpot and went on scratching. "Of course. I need to get everything from today down or I'll forget."

Resigned, Miri wearily pulled on her boots. "I need some air."

Rila narrated after her. "'Miri staggered out of her tent to get some air, and hopefully find Captain Kariss on watch.'"

"What?" Miri, who'd been halfway out, shot back in. Rila merely smirked as she went back for more ink.

"I told you, I have to get everything."

"This is what you're writing about?" Miri hissed, horrified, and wondering how much "everything" meant. "I thought this was about the expedition for 'posterity's sake', not about me liking... not that I do. I just..."

Rila shrugged and flipped through her pages. "It is. But nobody really wants to read some boring journey log. It's juicy bits like this that'll really sell." Choosing a few pages, oblivious to her friend's discomfort, she read.

"'Miri marveled as the Captain gracefully beheaded the attacking goblin.' Or 'Miri's heart was hammering, both from the shock of nearly falling to her death, and the lingering warmth of the Captain's hand on hers as she pulled her to safety.' Or 'Miri watched the Captain leave, admiring how her trousers looked so snug in all the right places.' Or how about—"

But Miri was already scrambling out of the tent, her hands over her ears, and promising to never drink with Rila again.

Rila shrugged. "Shame, I was just getting to the good part." She dipped her quill again and went back to writing.

"'Miri is rather pretty, I suppose," said the Captain, a faint blush rising in her cheeks.'"

IT'S WHAT'S INSIDE THAT COUNTS

NATHAN ALLING LONG (297 WORDS)

Honorable Mention

The list of every queer resistance member, human and non-humans alike, was contained in the tiny plastic bottle of smart ink. It only needed to be punctured and poured out onto a surface—any surface—to be revealed.

The bottle was wedged neatly between Flex's cheek and gums, and he tried not to tongue it as he walked toward security.

Flex was flagged, as expected. Only once on board, with the ship in the air, would he be safe. Until then, Flex had to stay calm, use charm. He recalled the thought that had amused him all morning: *I've never had so many queer folks in my mouth at once!*

But security didn't appreciate the smile. They riffled through Flex's bag, scanning it twice, then made Flex strip.

"Gladly," Flex said, the smile still sealed on his face.

After scanning his body, they let him get dressed, gave him back his bag.

"You can go," the commander said, "after you open your mouth."

Flex moved his lips as though to speak, then closed them tight. In the gesture, he managed to shift the bottle between his molars and clamp down. The liquid spread in his mouth, but Flex quickly swallowed it, along with the plastic.

Then Flex opened wide.

The flashlight peering into him was so bright, he felt the heat. He hoped he'd swallowed all the ink, that no name was drying on the roof of his mouth.

Finally, the commander, disappointed, said, "You can go."

Flex got on board and took a seat, still smiling.

Not until after take-off did he cry quietly to himself, thinking of the partners he'd never see again—for to get the invaluable list, the resistance would have to cut him open and carefully dry out his stomach and guts.

A PRISONER AND A CAPTAIN

B. EYRE (299 WORDS)

I draw myself as a man venturing across the seas far from the prison of my reality; twenty years served before violent execution. His image echoes throughout my imagination, a hero to keep me sane on days when Sister Mayim doesn't visit.

"Clara?" I remember shuddering before she corrected herself, "James."

She teaches me to escape, one word at a time, often leaving books from her personal library. Her letters are conservative, but they reveal more of her true nature. I draw her as a golden-haired nereid, perhaps a glimpse of her true form, company for my captain on long voyages.

"I want to get married," she whispers in my ear. "Do you?"

I nod my head in agreement; in ink, we exchanged solemn vows. The captain weds her on his ship at sunset. At sea, their years together pass quickly, but time moves slowly as Mayim visits become sporadic. In our last hours, she brings a bag for the captain and his family. She gives me poison.

"I wish we were them," I tell her while downing the vial. I lay down, and she combs my long hair with her fingers as we wait.

Hours pass as each heartbeat ricochets in my chest; as I stand, I can feel the room swaying. Quickly, I ran to the door; the air wasn't stagnant. In amazement, I hear waves and see the sky.

"James," I hear Mayim's voice in the breeze. It comes from above me.

"What happened?" I hear a man's voice leave my lips.

"I don't know," she holds a sleeping boy in her arms. "But he looks like you."

"This can't be possible. He's the captain's son from my drawings," Mayim's stomach has a protruding bump.

"I think he's our son," she smirks. "His name is Thomas."

CURSEBREAKER
BROOKE PRADO (297 WORDS)

Duncan leaned back and let out a hiss, tattooing needle held lightly in one hand while the other tensed against the chest of the man in his seat, who had just tried to sit up and with a nervously joking voice asked, "That bad?"

It was difficult not to smile at the young man—he was rather cute after all, which was likely what had brought him here, reeking of a curse like the alleyway behind Duncan's shop reeked of piss—and lie to him. That would only make what came next all the more difficult.

"I've seen worse," Duncan said, composing himself. "But not by much."

The man in his seat let his false bravado slip. "You c-can fix it?"

Duncan let out a snort, finding his jar of numbing cream. He whispered an incantation into it, fingers dipping in, before spreading it onto the tattoo that decorated the upper half of the other man's arm. The curse beneath the mark answered in turn, with what looked like fingertips pushing up from beneath the image. "Nah. I break these things."

The young man jolted up again with a sharp yelp, and Duncan held a hand to his chest again. The touch left shiny smears on his shirt front.

"Easy, Hazell," Duncan said, hoping the name was right. Hazell relaxed, so it must have been. "Ready?

"No."

Duncan pressed the needle down, and met tension both physical and mystical. He worked with ruthless efficiency, until the name of whatever angry ex-lover Hazell had broken the heart of disappeared beneath ink that shone like liquid moonlight.

When it was done, Hazell folded forward with a gasp. Beside him, Duncan finally smiled and patted him on the back.

"Moral of the story? Don't get tattoos of your boyfriend's name."

COLOURS OF UNION

L.S. REINHOLT (299 WORDS)

Winner - Second Place

Silgin had walked the path from the town of Solde to the magi's tower before. The first time, when Silgin was barely ten summers old, they had followed their aunt and her mate. A year after, their parents as they welcomed a new partner into their marriage. Later there had been cousins, siblings, friends, all walking the path with their chosen partners or mates up the steep slope to the old, crumbling tower in which the magi lived and studied.

Silgin had watched, always in awe, as the attendants had carried forth colourful jars from which a magus would siphon shimmering ink with a wand and then draw upon the skin of the people wishing to show their union. The colours, symbols and patterns were unique to each relationship and were said to tell the story of their love and devotion to those who knew how to read them.

Silgin just thought they were beautiful.

As a child they had believed that the ink held a spell that truly tied the people together and that they could not part unless it was somehow erased from their skin. But their grandmother, who had been with five different people over the years, had explained it worked the other way around:

If people chose to break the union, the ink would fade along with the feelings that had bound it.

And now Silgin was once again walking the path, but this time there was no one in front of them. They were going to get their own colours of union.

The young magus greeted them with a brilliant smile and gestured for Silgin to take a seat.

"Let the world see and recognise," she intoned, dipping her wand into a jar of sparkling emerald ink, "your union of one, Silgin of Solde."

The judges chose this story for one of the top three spots in part because the way the queer representation was so beautifully woven into such a small tale. They also loved the way the ace/aro character union of one was simply a part of life in the world.

SCIENCE FICTION PART THREE

"When people ask me to define science fiction and fantasy I say they are the literatures that explore the fact that we are toolmakers and users, and are always changing our environment."

— NALO HOPKINSON

PANDORA'S ROW

BY JASIE GALE (300 WORDS)

I find her at the end of Pandora's Row, her black tent crammed in amidst the fortune tellers and vendors selling relics and snake oil elixirs. Blue powder stains the earth, and incense laces the exhaust billowing in from the skyport where I've moored my shuttle.

"Took you long enough," she snarls as I enter.

A single lantern hangs over a table carved with runes from a long-dead planet. Some say she was the only survivor, scraped up from the world's waning ocean floor along with other forgotten treasures.

Onyx eyes drop to the pouch at my hip, and her tongue darts out, teasing the corner of her mouth. "If you're here, you know my price."

I set the pouch on the table, and greedy, ink-stained fingers inspect my payment. The bivalves are the size of a fist with barbed spines. My hands are scarred from harvesting them, but she easily cracks one open with her teeth and devours the writhing muscle inside. A clicking purr rattles in her throat. It sets my nerves on edge, but I don't shy away when she looks up at me, her tongue lapping the iridescent nacre inside the shell.

"What'll it be?" she hisses. "Wings? Claws?"

"No."

"Scales? Tusks?" She cackles. "Oh, the things you men ask of me."

"I'm no man," I say, bristling as her reptilian eyes search mine.

"So I see." She clutches the pouch of bivalves to her breast. "Undress and lie down."

I've not removed my tunic for anyone in a very long time, but I do as instructed.

Her fingers are cold on my back, tracing runes down my spine. My flesh drinks up the ink, absorbing the spell. Until I feel it emerge. My *true* form—more magnificent than any wings or claws.

Free at last.

THE FLIGHT OF THE TELORITES

LOU SYLVRE (300 WORDS)

When the government inked me, tattooing on a DNA progenitive blue that carried telomere and "repair code" gene tags, I'd been a soldier deployed to the Mojave ground war.

"So we can track you in the desert," they lied. Not that they needed to explain—Lab rats have no choice.

The ink worked, but only for those of us who had another "key" present in our genes—a sequence long eradicated in the inbred, DNA-manipulated, Preeminite ruling class.

Long telomeres plus self-repair equals long lifespan. Long life equals wealth. Wealth equals power, and power is for Preeminites.

They failed, and they feared the "Telorite monsters" they'd created. Military guards and barbed wire surrounded Telorite compounds. They raided sporadically, taking anything they didn't want us to have.

Last month, they took children.

In two lifetimes I'd collected eight men and women as co-mates, as many children as birthdays, and more enemies than both those totals combined. Still, I was respected in my compound. When a decision was needed, the others gathered and waited for my word.

Thomas, my oldest friend and favored lover, stepped into my workshop, his face ashen. "John… You saw the news?"

I shivered with premonition. "No."

"They tested the kids."

We already knew what they'd found. Our children were like us—mutants—even showing "wandering ink," as the army had called the blue streaking the whites of our eyes.

"Exterminate," Tommy choked. "That's what they said."

I rose, took his hand, and led him out to the plaza.

To the gathered people, I said, "We have choices. Give in—let them end our nightmare. Fight—surely futile."

But we'd guessed this day would come—planned, studied, thieved parts and supplies. Built a starship.

I smiled. "Instead, let's pack for a long trip."

Skyward, the stars twinkled a welcome.

TO HAVE AND TO HOLD AND TO HOLD AND TO HOLD

M.X. KELLY (299 WORDS)

Honorable Mention

Rna'la arrived at Intergalactic Date-A-Thon and signed in using zir own gelatinous fluid (no scratchy ballpoint for zem, thanks!) The human woman collecting signatures blushed pinkly. Rna'la's hearts throbbed in zir throat. *Probably not attending.*

Ze passed several individuals in the hallway. Some bowed, some ignored zem. Not everyone recognized the current ruler of Th'ul.

Rna'la reached zir reserved room, the sign reading:

LEADER OF HOUSE TH'UL (YES, THAT One) & *Tattoo Artist, Seeking Wives to Help Expand Realm (No Devouring). Free tats for long, interesting conversations.*

FIRST INQUIRER: human male... *Either can't read or an asshole.*

"If you mate, can I watch?"

Asshole, then. Rna'la licked zir face-feelers threateningly. He left... quickly.

Later, four women came together: a reptilian Marusian, two bird-like Djoras, one raven-haired human.

Humans fascinated Rna'la. When Th'ulians found Earth, seeking zir long lost uncle, they discovered an entire mythology about him there. Despite their terror, they helped recover Cth from his deep-sea cryosleep chamber.

I could procreate with the Marusian. Similar anatomy... Doctor said my mating implant is functional now.

THEY WERE FANTASTIC CONVERSATIONALISTS. The human not at all frightened. When Rna'la asked what she wanted, she said: "A heart, over my heart, with your name in it and your tentacles wiggling behind..." Her friends giggled. She blushed. Startled, Rna'la realized she was the woman from the sign-in booth. Zir implant began dripping.

Her friends removed their shirts. "We'd like the same."

Hard and dripping. Rna'la attached the tattoo gun to the inkwells…

Eighteen months later, they all stood before the Th'ulian High Priest. He began, "Do you, Rna'la, take these persons...to have and to hold, and to hold, and to hold?"

Rna'la leaned on zir fully erect mating arm implant and waved zir tentacles.

"I do, I do, I do, and I do!"

ODDITIES
NAOMI TAJEDLER (292 WORDS)

Honorable Mention

Ever since their first arrival on Earth, Oddities have successfully built a symbiotic relationship with the Human race.

Their ink-like fluidity allows them to run through the human system, manifesting unspoken emotions, needs and wishes through glyphs and pictures at first, before adapting to Universel.

As interesting as they may be as species and companions, though, Professor Margaw would like to remind his own Oddity that it is not polite to show up in public on his forehead to proclaim an adoring lust for Doctor Terrepc'h.

No, it doesn't matter that his outfit is particularly flattering.

This tsa'if and ch'ultza are really amaz—

No, stop, no more poems appearing on his forehead to celebrate Terrepc'h's ethereal beauty!

The symbiote does stop, as reluctant as it is to do so, but it starts a rhythm in Margaw's veins, doubling up his heartbeat.

A tentative glance in Terrepc'h's direction answers Margaw's wonderment.

For the honorable doctor's Oddity is responding to him.

No words, no glyphs, no symbols mark the doctor's tan skin. Instead, brushstrokes of colors move across his cheeks and nose before diving down his neck and below the collar of his tsa'if before reappearing on his wrists.

How Margaw longs to follow that path with his touch, with his fingers and tongue and whole self …!

A blush that has nothing to do with his Oddity spreads on Terrepc'h's cheeks as he looks away from Margaw.

Could it be that their inked oddities have shown them that they were behaving like besotted idiots?

Perhaps.

But for now, Professor Margaw needs to take that first step to move from the world of unspoken desires to the world of expressed interest.

Now would be a good time for his Oddity to help him out!

THE MORNING AFTER

RAINE NORMAN (300 WORDS)

Zach woke to his head and arse throbbing in time with his pulse. He'd had a hook up last night with much shagging and alcohol involved no doubt. Prising open his eyes, left first then right, a veritable Adonis with bed hair and stubbled chin lay beside him.

Zach tried to recall the bloke's name. Nope. Nothing. Shit. And it wasn't the first time with him either.

Deciding he needed a shower and a piss but not necessarily in that order, Zach left the comfort of the bed and staggered to the bathroom. He pissed like a racehorse before turning on the shower and stepping in the cubicle before the water had warmed up. He washed his hair, then ran a soapy sponge over his body and yelped when he scrubbed his left buttock.

"That off-world git better not have bitten me."

Zach scowled. His taste for exotic types wasn't always the safest choice. The increasingly warm water started to really sting as it washed over his buttock. No. It began to properly bloody hurt! He twisted, but couldn't see anything so he stepped out of the shower, not caring about the water dripping everywhere and stood in front of the mirror, becoming aware of a bluish hue to the light in the room.

"What the hell?"

Hsilgne

Not only was there bloody blue writing on his arse, but it was glowing! He turned out the bathroom light and to his horror the light emanating from his buttock grew brighter.

A chuckle from the other room.

"You will not forget my name again. My ink will not fade. See you next cycle."

Before Zach could react, he heard footsteps and the door to his flat opening and closing.

Shit! He'd married the alien sod! The Detinu always marked their spouses.

THE PRESENT
MONIQUE CUILLERIER (300 WORDS)

Gwen left Earth with nothing but a small bottle of green ink.

Veronica had wanted nothing else for her birthday. It had been a long time since she had ink for her fountain pen. These days it was difficult to find and expensive when you did.

Gwen and Veronica did not have much to spare.

They were a practical couple. But in the evenings, as they sat in front of the fireplace and Veronica wrote in her journal with a pencil stub, she would speak wistfully of the ink that reminded her of childhood.

Helpless in the face of Veronica's wishes, Gwen scrimped and saved. And one afternoon, a few days before Veronica's birthday, Gwen took a bus into the city.

The ink was perfect, a deep emerald ink that glowed when light shone through it.

Walking back to the bus stop, Gwen heard a deep rumble above and raised her eyes. When they found a hulking grey spaceship, her mind told her to run, but she stood and stared. The ship sunk to the ground and extended a ramp. Too shocked to resist, Gwen was swept aboard with those around her.

Communication with the aliens was frustrating, but eventually they conveyed the danger they had rescued the humans from, an asteroid headed towards Earth.

The aliens hadn't saved everyone, but they had done what they could. And now their overfull ships lurched towards a planet where they promised the humans would be safe.

Gwen decided to take the aliens at their word. After all, she was a practical person.

And she chose to trust that Veronica was on one of the other ships. That was, perhaps, less practical.

Each night, Gwen dreamed of a fireplace and a sofa and Veronica writing in her journal in green ink.

UNFAMILIAR WATERS
FOSTER BRIDGET CASSIDY (300 WORDS)

Honorable Mention

I pressed my palm to the window and gazed out at the dark expanse. Small lights twinkled off in the distance—millions of light years away. The stretch of black reminded me of home.

I turned from the window. Pearl curled up in a bed of kelp and I smiled. In her sleep, she clutched the eggs we'd deposited. Half hers; half mine. Who fathered our children didn't matter. We would raise our young together. Traveling with eggs was worth the risk if it meant our happiness on another world.

The ship lurched and the motion roused Pearl from her slumber.

"Venus?" she called drowsily.

"Yes, dear?"

She stretched. As she lowered her hand, she realized she'd gathered the eggs around her.

"They don't need heat yet," she said instead of sharing vivid images from her dream. As our colony's soothsayer, her connection to our ancestors kept us safe. She rubbed at her inked moon—tattooed on her forehead at birth.

"They're fine," I insisted, going to her. I gently scooped up an egg. I held it to the light and saw a shape wiggle inside. Our child. "Tell me of your vision."

"I saw you, strong and brave, leading our people into unfamiliar waters."

"Soon?"

"Yes."

Here, our eggs stood a better chance of survival. Perhaps ten would live. Would it be this little one? Steadfast like me? Marked like Pearl?

I set the egg down with their siblings. "Only another year of travel." I turned back to the window.

Pearl flicked her tail, and grabbed my hand on her way to the wall. She tugged on me.

We slid through the water and, together, peered at the far away lights. Pearl's visions led us somewhere. We set out on faith; we would finish that way.

As a family.

FREE HUGS
PAULA MCGRATH (300 WORDS)

Marion coughed as she stepped out of the airlock onto Space-station 897. The air stank like wet laundry left in the dryer too long. After three long years she finally had some leave, and she wanted a tattoo to commemorate it.

This system's sentient lifeform were asexual humanoids with tentacles, and they had a gorgeous written language. She wanted a tattoo that said 'Three Years'. Prosaic, yes, but in this alien script even the word for faeces was worth framing.

The tattooist sucked on a nic-stick as they listened to Marion explain what she wanted. Their dubious expression didn't give Marion much confidence, but it was too late now. She hid her revulsion at their touch, afraid it would be misconstrued. It wasn't that she was revolted by their particular touch, she didn't like anybody touching her. Marion was so glad her next contract was in deep space where she could be alone with the AI for 9 months of blissful solitude.

Two hours of constant pain later...

'All done,' said the tattooist with a wink, 'good for a lifetime plus two weeks.'

Marion nodded and waved her wrist over the APM, feeling floaty.

She walked out of the parlour in a euphoric daze, admiring her new tattoo. The script was gorgeous, all flowing lines and flourishes. She heard a strange squeal and looked up. A humungous, local sapient was approaching, tentacles flailing.

Before she could do anything, she was engulfed. It felt like a handsy boa constrictor and his drunk friend.

'I can't breathe,' she wheezed, trying to push it away.

The sapient replied in its own tongue, a high-pitched squeal.

'Help!' Marion squeaked, fighting panic.

'L'lon doesn't speak Terran,' explained the other alien. 'It's just taking what you offered.'

'What's that?'

It pointed at her tattoo.

'Free Hugs.'

SOULINK
AVA KELLY (296 WORDS)

Winner - First Place

The SOULink Forum

Welcome to the largest support forum in the Free Station Coalition for those struggling with their soulmarks. Make sure to read the rules before you post. Be kind!

SOULink > Astara Space Station Subforum > Soulmarks

Thread: **Double-zero ink issue** – *Last updated SOL 9812:71:49 – Started by Inkless64*

Inkless64 – *New member – Posted on SOL 9811:05:32*

Hi. I'm new here, but hopefully you can help me. I recently found one of my two soulmates. I put myself in the database and got a match! They also live on Astara, and this would be joyous under different circumstances. You see, both of my marks are on my right wrist. Which means I have two platonic soulmates, yeah? And that suits me fine, but... My soulmate's matching one is on their left. Is something wrong with me? I don't know what to do.

SpaceRock – *Senior member – Reply on SOL 9811:06:88*

Could this finally be a duplicate?

Jaxster – *Moderator* – *Reply on SOL 9811:08:12*

Nope. Scientifically proven no duplicates are possible. Elements, yes. Whole mark, no.

Jaxster – *Moderator* – *Reply on SOL 9811:08:23*

Hi, welcome.
THERE'S NOTHING WRONG WITH YOU.
There are many out there without romantic and many without platonic (like me) marks. The match exists for a reason. You won't know for sure until you ask them, but here's a possibility: they might be lithromantic. They might not want reciprocation.
Don't let this discourage you. If it does turn out your soulmate's an asshole, we're here for you. We also have a monthly in-person meeting for Astarians.

Inkless64 – *New member* – *Reply on SOL 9812:71:49*

Jaxster, thank you so much! I replied to the match and guess what. You were right! I'm crying a little. And laughing a lot. We'd both like to join the meetings.
Happy souls,
Inkless

The judges loved this story, both for its unusual format and for its heartfelt ace representation. One judge in particular praised its modern updating of an old story form, the epistolary tale (stories told through an exchange of letters). And the judges loved the story's flawless authenticity which kept "Soullink" from feeling gimmicky.

ROUGH DRAFT #9/GROCERY LIST
MAGALY GARCIA (294 WORDS)

Dear mom,

~~Fuck you.~~

I deserve a tree branch from your orange tree. You got it from abuelita's tree, who received a branch from her papi's, who was gifted one from his mami, and so on. ~~For centuries,~~ It has been our family's way of remembering our ancestors' faces by growing oranges with our bodies' compost, especially since half of them never learned how to read or write. To let that tradition die just because you disapprove of my marriage with Ximena is to allow our family history ~~of becoming part of the tree upon death and returning as food for our loved ones~~ to die.

La amo, mami. Abuelita would have loved to know Ximena and I fell in love. She did say Ximena would make a good wife someday because she can make sweet tamales from scratch.

Please, think of abuelita. She was your mom. Don't you want my future children to see her and the rest of the family someday? Even if it's just their faces on the skins of our oranges?

~~Do you want to throw away all your hard work, from crossing the Rio Grande River with only your orange tree branch~~

~~Remember when I was five and you asked me to someday turn your body into our family compost for your orange~~

~~Written word and my memories alone won't~~

~~When you someday pass away, I don't want your ashes spread in the ocean. I want to see your face grow from the tree right next to abuelita, so I can tell my children how you left home for her. For me. For them.~~

. . .

~~Te amo,~~
 ~~I miss you,~~
 Your daughter,
 Nayeli

Buy: *pens (this one's getting dry), envelopes, dog food, tampons, Hot Cheetos, postage stamps, bottom shelf wine*

OFF-SPECTRUM

KELLY HAWORTH (295 WORDS)

The humidity increases, and I start to coalesce. I float through cirrostratus level, past Ultramarine and Crimson, tendrils of their nebulous forms wafting in greeting. I waft back, my gray shade growing denser by the moment.

I'm not sure I'm ready.

Even though I've thought about it, during the long hours in altocumulus level, bending jet streams toward hungry turbines.

Even though I've dreamed about it, drifting up where the atmosphere's thin enough that radiation sets me alight. Staring into dark black abyss, counting every star.

But there's more to me than a color. More to me than a name.

When they had said, 'you could be anything,' they hadn't really meant it. They meant, you could be in these wavelength ranges, like everyone else. We don't speak about in-betweens. How many Chartreuses are there? Periwinkles? The gaps in the spectrum stand out.

Yet, deep inside me, in my structure, I know what I want.

Now to somehow find courage to own it.

Nimbostratus level looms close, and every wisp of me is thick, weighted. Canary brushes past me, their form billowing with attempted encouragement, but I only see concern.

I pull tightly into myself, and enter the Nim.

Inside, the weight of countless molecules and immense moisture transforms my dark particles into liquid. I rain down, and splash onto an outcropping of rock.

I observe the small crowd, analyzing wavelength after wavelength. So many are within strict values.

But some…

Some are like me.

My wavelength and thoughts align, and my now-liquid form reaches out to an ancient tome before me, touches its porous pages, and leaves a mark with my own substance. A scrawl with the ink of me. My new identity.

"Lavender."

I vibrate with pride. Around me, in-betweens vibrate pride back.

THE TATTOOIST

JESSICA M. KORMOS (275 WORDS)

There was no going back once the needle touched your skin. Fayola went first. Our husband, Kang-dae, sat on her left and I on her right as the needles rapidly etched her skin with the alien creature's ink. Her skin began to bubble, glowing like pearls, as The Tattooist went to work adding our names to her body. My name first, Aria. Kang-dae. Fayola. Indigo, our child's chosen name.

In the end, this wasn't a hard decision. We knew the risks with the ink; everyone did by that point. And no one cared. Once the truth came out that we were not colonists, but cartographers, it didn't take long for our starcraft to go feral. Then we found the creature, dead in one of our solar sails. The being that would allow us to transcend, and to escape our metal prison. Every day more of the crew went missing; more random airlock alarms went off at all hours. And Indigo was already out among the stars, waiting for us.

Once Kang-dae and I were similarly inked, The Tattooist walked us to the airlock. "You're Indigo's family."

We all nodded.

"They'll be so happy to see you again." She pressed the forged security clearance into my hand, turned on her heels, and left without a word.

Inside the airlock our transformations progressed rapidly. In mere minutes we'd sloughed off most of our humanity. Our tattoos remained as we phase shifted, the silky caress of other universes brushing up against our new interdimensional shapes. Through the static, I heard the voice of my flesh.

"Mama." Indigo's voice in my ear. "I've missed you."

I opened the airlock.

PARANORMAL PART TWO

"Violence is never the answer but sometimes, like with cockroaches, it is the only possible response."

— Tanya Huff

ALTERNATE ENDINGS

JORANE G. BARTON (294 WORDS)

Joey rolled over in bed and checked the time on her phone. The blue light made her eyes ache. Dark still. She kicked the bed covers off with her feet, and sat up. The hands were getting worse, and she gave them a good shake. Gotta get the blood flowing. She'd absorbed Mel's ailments along with her gifts and time was running out. Joey wrestled on her robe and padded through the dark hallway. Thermostat, light switch, stiff fingers thawing out against a mug of hot coffee. Back at her desk the inkwell was nearly dry. Everything was running out. She'd have to choose her words carefully and work quickly this time. The original story ended with Mel in the truck. It was a wonder she'd manage to rig the hose that way. She was too good at everything. Joey arrived almost in time. A black truck on a dark street, lights off, engine still running. Brain gone, heart stopped. But the soul lingered. It glowed softly in her lovely face. The incantation left Joey's lips, and she prayed she'd said it correctly. She winced slicing into Mel's wrist, and collected the blood into the inkwell that had belonged to Mel's grandmother. Mel tried to hide that from her too, but she hadn't tried hard enough. Just a quick and dirty locator spell and that was all it took. The truck had been a bit harder to find but still. With Mel's inkwell there was hope. A deep breath, and Joey began. Dipping the quill into the ink and pressing the tip to the parchment. Yesterday she'd fucked it up and she had just enough left for one more try. She had to get it right this time. They both deserved a happy ending.

THE COLORS OF FATE
GENEVA VAND (298 WORDS)

Honorable Mention

I get out of the shower and it's there. Dripping down the mirror—*splip*—and forming a rivulet of color across the tile floor. Thinner than paint, more vibrant than water. Sometimes it's iridescent, but today it's just...*bright*. A stream of colorful consciousness leading me across the bathroom, down the hall, out of...wait.

I go to my bedroom and hastily put on whatever I can reach. Yesterday's bra, the jeans from the floor, finger comb my short hair, a random t-shirt—purple. The same color the ink is today. Does that mean something?

Probably not.

I stuff my feet into shoes and hurry out of my apartment and down the sidewalk. I barely remember to pocket my keys and wallet and lock the door.

Where will the ink take me this time? A lost pet? A kid? Once it had been a homeless man with pneumonia. Once a teenaged girl who'd gotten lost. But there was also the time it was just a really good sale on my favorite jeans.

I slow as the stream thickens and look around. A coffee shop? *My* coffee shop? What could possibly be here?

I follow the stream of ink through the crosswalk and between the outdoor tables. It pools under someone's feet. My eyes follow the legs up to a body, a face.

Her eyes meet mine, wide and surprised. Happy. Shockingly blue.

I drift closer.

I sit at her table and she reaches for me. I let her touch me, and she rubs her finger over my cheek. When she pulls her hand away, she shows me a smear of shimmering turquoise...ink.

But it's purple today. Isn't it?

She smiles and the turquoise disappears, melting into her skin. "I'm Emily."

"Becca.

"Will you have coffee with me, lovely Becca?"

"Yes."

THE ANGEL WITH DEMON BLOOD

LILY LUCHESI (300 WORDS)

I didn't think Ananiel was going to wake up.

My angel, my crazy, brave, loyal angel. They tossed aside Heaven to save me from Hell, and in doing so, is now on life support, being fed as much spare grace as I managed to steal during the battle.

If they never woke up, it would be my fault.

"Diana," called my little brother. "You can permanently replace the grace Ananiel lost."

I looked up at him, confused. "How?"

He smiled. "Ink."

I looked down at my tattoos, over at Ananiel's scarred body.

"Your tattoos don't come from the ink humans use," he explained. "They're from your blood."

I knew that, but… "How do I use that to help Ana?"

"Do you remember the last thing they said before they fell?"

Of course I did.

"As long as I can be with you, in whatever capacity, I will be happy."

"You'll subvert their angelic powers, entwine them with yours. Ananiel will become a hybrid, bound to that body forever. But they will wake and heal," Jericho said.

So I tried.

My right index fingernail elongated and thinned, turning into a black, needlelike tool. Gently, I took their left hand in mine and pressed my nail into their skin. My blood, my demonic essence, flowed from my body and into Ananiel's skin.

I drew flowers, stars, vines. Beautiful things. I tattooed all night, until their arm was covered in ink. When I reached their heart, their ice blue eyes opened, the whites turning black.

At the same time, we said, "You saved me."

Ananiel pulled me down into a kiss.

"You're not mad?" I asked.

They shook their head. "My blood doesn't matter. I am still me, and I am here with you. I can create a new Heaven here, with you."

LOVE'S PORTRAIT

K.S. MURPHY (300 WORDS)

"You understand," Teaghan said, "what it means should you fail to break the curse."

Nerves danced in Hollis's eyes as they peered at the Dark Prince through thick lashes. Teaghan offered a grin and slid his hand across their cheek, framing it in his palm. He smelled Hollis's fear. It saturated the room and sent a pleasant shiver down Teaghan's spine.

"I do," Hollis whispered, nuzzling against Teaghan's hand. "I love you, Teaghan."

"And you are here with me of your own accord?"

"I am."

Teaghan smiled. Pressed a kiss to Hollis's brow. Said, "I love you, too, Hollis. It's time."

Hollis nodded and took a deep breath. This did nothing to lessen their fear, but humans often liked to pretend.

"I'm ready."

On the other end of his bedroom was an ornate gilded frame surrounding a blank canvas. A small wooden table with a glass inkwell and quill sat in front of it.

Teaghan handed Hollis the quill and, tender and gentle, held their hand as they pricked their fingertip with it, producing a single drop of red blood. Hollis dipped the quill into the inkwell. Hand still and steady, they smeared the faery ink across the canvas.

They waited with bated breath.

When nothing happened, Teaghan dared an exhilarated exhale. Until Hollis, eyes wide with terror, dropped the quill. Panic. A blood-curdling cry as their body slowly and painfully dissolved to ink and was absorbed into the canvas.

Teaghan sighed and gazed at the image forever sealed within the frame.

The curse hadn't lifted.

And he'd lost another.

"Shall I hang this in the hall," asked his servant, "with the others?"

"No." Teaghan hung Hollis's portrait next to his bed. "I really loved this one."

The Dark Prince had loved them all.

He would search for another tomorrow.

FOR DEATH DOESN'T PART

TAYLOR ROTH (298 WORDS)

Dying can be painful, however, after experiencing it twenty times Pen would describe death as not so bad. Lately, the most painful part was waking up to their partner's grimace afterward.

Pen awoke with a grin not surprised to see the grim reaper before them. "Babe! You'll never-"

The embodiment of death sighed and stopped Pen's story. Death knew they couldn't keep this up. It broke every rule they'd agreed to in the beginning and they stood to lose everything. "We need to talk."

Pen's smile dissipated as they braced for bad news.

"This is the last time I can bring you back."

Pen had heard Death say this before, but this time felt different in its finality. "For reals, huh?"

Death nodded.

"So, what your plan then?"

"As I see it. You have two options, my love."

"Well, option one is to die for good, right? Boo. I vetoed it. Next option, please."

"Now, you must not answer hastily for it is not an option that I would even wish upon my worst enemy."

Pen watched a contract appear from thin air and looked to Death for an explanation.

"It would be unfair to not give you the option, but you will not get the pen until you've read it all the way through and understand its gravity. In fact, I will read through it with you." A second copy of the papers appeared in Death's hand along with the pen.

Reading the top of the contract was the only word Pen had decided they needed to read. Marriage.

Biting through their fingernail they used their own blood to sign it before Death could even begin to stop them.

Marrying Death was definitely a painful process, yet it was worth waking to their partner's smile every morning.

A DISH SERVED HOT

JACQUI GREAVES (295 WORDS)

You stare at the plate of darkness before you. I've truly put my heart and soul into preparing this special dish for you, I say. It's not a lie. You take my words at face value, and the scales of your tail shimmer with glee. I flutter my wings so they, too, fluoresce.

You twirl the fork, winding black strands into a mouthful that disappears—sucked between your coral lips. My nipples tighten at the memory of those lips on my cunt, while my tongue teased your mermaid pearl. You tasted of oysters and said I smelled of roses. I still love you.

Your eyes change from sea-green to lagoon-blue, sparkling with sunlight. You smile wide—serrated teeth pearlescent white. Squid, you announce with your delicious lisp. This is the game we play. I create dishes blended from our worlds, and you guess the ingredients.

You're not specific enough, I insist. You suck down another mouthful, then sink below the surface. Your remora adjusts its position. No cheating, I shout. A school of tiny silver fish retreats into your billowing hair at the sound of my voice.

Ripples spread as you rise above the surface to join me in the air. There's squid ink in both the pasta and the sauce, you say. You also taste wine and tomatoes, but there is something else. Something new you've never tasted before.

I fan my wings and rise in the air. My maw widens, transforming my sweet smile into the fearsome sharp-toothed grimace of an enraged fairy.

Black garlic, I say, and lots of it. Your eyes change to stormy-grey and your scales lose their glimmer. With a flip of your tail, you're gone.

I hope that vampire bitch you're fucking enjoys it, I shout behind you.

TOLD
RODELLO SANTOS (299 WORDS)

Honorable Mention

DIRECTOR'S CHOICE - J. Scott Coatsworth

An interviewer once asked my mom where she got her plotlines.

"Witchcraft. I summon story-spirits who petition me to write them."

The interviewer had laughed. "Well, who wouldn't want to work with a bestselling author?"

"Exactly."

That's when I knew she'd sold out. Stories should come from *inside* us. Whatevs.

My opinion of story-spirits hardly improved when a stray one entered my room, oblivious that a teenager's space was sacrosanct. I slammed my laptop shut.

"Wrong room," I growled.

We matched in age, gender. His fashion screamed post-apocalyptic— dark, dust-streaked survival-wear. Conflict haunted his face: keening, resigned; proud, vulnerable. Cute, if I'm being honest.

"I was h-hoping you could put in a good word. To your mom."

I snorted. "Dude, she *loathes* YA dystopian."

He flinched, face darkening. "Is that all you see? These clothes, my world? They're trappings. I'm not just a goddamn genre."

Guilt shut me up.

I understood labels— "Fag!" "Flip!" Being branded at a glance.

He approached. This close, I realized every line of him, every blush, contour, was lettering, his inky hair a wilderness of sentences, his expression a literal amalgam of expressions. Amber-dark eyes glimmered, indelible.

His nearness—present, tense—alters my perspective. His longing radiates warmth.

A rough draft outlines his jaw. Self-conscious, I read his lips, his neck. I circle around him, following a prologue. Where I stare, clothes unravel into excerpts upon bare skin. An exposition.

All the while, he's reading me too.

His interrobang-filled smile dies when I repeat myself: "My mom doesn't write dystopia. I'm sorry."

"I just want to be told."

"I...understand."

Tears smudge words in their wake, but my fingertips absorb the blotting on his cheek.

"Luckily,"—I open my laptop, delete the embarrassingly uninspired draft I'd started— "she's not the only writer in the family."

There was stiff competition for my Director's Choice this year. I started with ten stories, each of which had something I adored. It took a while, but in the end, Told's *combination of a writing theme, a plucky protagonist, and a truly lovely, lyrical storytelling style won me over. The beauty of the flowing text and the idea of the story dying to be told and made flesh proved too much for me to resist. I hope you enjoyed it as much as I did.*

—*J. Scott Coatsworth*

THE PEN IS MIGHTIER
KAJE HARPER (298 WORDS)

The scent of smoke rose as he set pen to paper.

Yes. Burn. You deserve it.

He inscribed each letter precisely, sending pulses of power into the silver nib.

> **Dear not-so-dear Stephen,**
>
> *You want to have your wedding cake and eat me too. To turn from our secret bed to your unsuspecting bride and play the man of honor. While having none.*
>
> *But I'm not a man to be trifled with. As you read this, you may notice a sudden heat, a burn that gathers down there, where I've touched you so many times. Is it intensifying? Pain eclipsing desire? Do you feel my wrath—*

A flicker of flame raced over his lines, the words blackening. He cursed and lifted the pen, beating at the paper with a rag. Extinguishing the embers took several strokes, and he frowned at the tatters and ash that remained.

All that anger and pain, reduced to black smears and the words, *Dear not-so-dear Stephen, You—*

You.

He set the pen into its stand, his hand shaking.

You. Whom I loved. But who loved wealth and advancement more.

He held Stephen's fate in his sodomite hands. He could ruin him publicly, if he were willing to destroy himself too. That bride's wealthy family would turn away in disgust, Stephen's club would blackball him. But he had no taste for using society rules he loathed as a weapon.

He touched the inkwell; the power within it hummed under his fingertips. *I would have offered him that power, if I'd truly trusted him.*

In my fears he might bring me to misuse it, I never pictured this.

He picked up a simple pencil.

Dear Stephen, go to hell.

Not as pointed as flaming balls, but words he could walk away from with his soul intact.

SHADOWBIRD
RJ MUSTAFA (300 WORDS)

With the ink spewing from my veins, I draw patterns.

My tongue swells, head spinning as the hunters guffaw. They brag about the fortune they'll make from selling me. Shame burns inside when my eyes meet the deep-brown of his. I curse myself—again—for falling under his spell.

Flames shimmer on his copper skin as Hamedu crouches before my cage. He grins; scents of desert fire and betrayal scorch my nostrils. I should've known not to trust a boy's pretty eyes when he showed at my doorstep, begging for shelter.

Lost in his stories, I forgot solitude. It didn't matter that he was human and I a night creature—Shadowbird, as they called us. Hamedu kissed my bearded chin. Our teeth clashed. I'd been starving, his touch igniting me. Too late, I tasted sunpoppy; his acolytes burst inside as I collapsed and imprisoned me.

"You've been silent, Djehu," he sneers.

Nauseous, I bite charred lips as black fluids slither out of the cage. I smirk; there's something they ignored about Shadowbirds.

When the moon makes way for infinite darkness, our blood sings with magic unknown to this world.

All I had to do was draw the score.

Shadows rouse, slashing as chatter turns to screams. My cage shatters. Hamedu's eyes burn with fury and something else as I stand.

His gaze softens, fingers sliding toward my neck in a treacherous embrace. I thrust the hidden blade aside as the slaughter ends.

Hamedu studies my bruised black skin and wine-colored eyes. He could slit my throat with the knife strapped inside his ankle, yet his will falters at the sight of my reawakened wings. Obsidian feathers float as my nose brushes his.

"Come with me," I whisper.

Hamedu trembles against my shoulder. His answer lingers long after I soar.

"Yes."

HEART INK

AMARILYS ACOSTA (298 WORDS)

Hurricane-force winds and icy rain jolt Michael and me from our cozy tangle. It takes us a moment to notice the sunny watercolor of Rio's beloved Puerto Rican shores above our headboard is now a violent spiral of greys and swaying palm trees.

Michael's worried eyes match mine.

It's been years since Rio lost control over their ink. Only danger—

Grabbing my knives from the bedside table, I rush out of our bedroom, hot on Michael's steps.

The canvases along the stairs—a tropical jungle, a sailboat, a Bomba festival—are alive with the same loud ferocity, displaying their painter's mood. On the first floor, the family room weathers the ink magic pouring from our wedding portrait.

A crack of lightning and a boom of thunder shake the walls.

Michael curses and summons his staff as we hurry outside.

My mind-link goes unanswered by Rio.

We flat-out run to the detached barn-turned-studio where they spend their mornings. When Michael tackles the door, he bounces off a shield.

I haul him up and knock instead. "Rio, please open up!"

A loud sob comes from inside and it cleaves my heart in three.

"Let us in, sweetheart."

"Whatever it is, we're in this together," Michael adds, clasping his hand with mine.

"Always."

We stand close to the door, ready to blast in and slay whatever demon—corporeal or emotional—haunts our Rio this morning.

But when Rio opens up, they greet us with a wide smile and teary eyes. "We did it."

"Did what?"

Rio chuckles and raises a plastic stick showing a plus sign on the tiny screen.

Michael's joyful grin definitely matches mine.

I let the knives fall, Michael vanishes the staff, and we both embrace Rio. The ink settles as we open our hearts for one more.

FANTASY PART FOUR

"Absolutes are absolutely dangerous."

— JAMES TIPTREE JR.

BABBLER

JOE BAUMANN (298 WORDS)

Honorable Mention

When he speaks, words pour out of Dex's mouth like blood, like cherry juice, staining his lips and teeth and chin, cutting across his throat, sliding down his sternum. They drizzle across his ribs, wants and needs and curses etching along the bones and muscles. They pool in his navel, a clot of letters and commas and semi-colons tangled like hair in a drain. His mother curses the stains on his sweaters and undershirts. His teachers berate him, his whispers to classmates announcing themselves against the collars of his polos. Eventually, Dex stops speaking. He learns ASL. He learns how to point, to speak with his eyes. Girls want him because he's broody. They want to taste the words as they fall from his lips. They imagine his moans taste like strawberries, currant.

Dex wants the girls, but he also wants Peter Scarbrough, who plays basketball, knotted calf muscles flayed and strong like cut-open hearts. He wants to cheer for Peter, but his mother makes him do his own laundry, pay for dry-cleaning and stain removers. So Dex sits in the stands and watches Peter's shoulders twitching as he sinks free throws, clapping but never hooting or yelling. He watches Peter hug the cheerleaders, pull their bodies close.

Sometimes, in the shower, Dex talks to himself, lips an open drain from which ink runs in strong gushes. He moves the words around on his body, turning *I hate you* into *I love you. Make it stop* into *This is me.* But by the time he turns off the water, he's washed his skin blank. And every night he hopes, prays, that he will find the right words, the right way to deliver them, so that the right people will want not a taste but instead want to listen.

AEDAN
HERMINIA ROOT (300 WORDS)

Something's been eating at me since last night. I blacked out, again, remember fuck all. Let a stranger give me a stick and poke, a little red lizard. Stupid, I know, but I am stupid, so whatever. The thing hurts like fuck in a way it shouldn't. I remember them saying they were an old hand and sterilizing the needle over a flame, but I also remember getting it on my arm and it's not there, so I don't know.

OK. LESS HUNGOVER. The more I remember the less sense it makes. All bruised from clumsily dancing to weird music (all bells?). Throat feels like I "smoked a grip of nettles," which, fine, I would. A lizard on my fucking chest when I know damn well I wasn't taking my shirt and binder off at a party full of strangers, no matter how drunk I was. Feels like it's biting into me. My skin's still crawling, all pins and needles (ha).

OK, but how could I just stumble into some bonfire and get a massive lizard tattoo on my chest? It's definitely growing. Still hurts, like it's gnawing at me. I make it a practice not to stand around staring at myself in the mirror, because fuck you, but I think it moved (again?). I can't even write what I'm thinking because I'm afraid I'll jinx it but maybe my vague images of some pretty out-there-looking partiers weren't just dream nonsense. I mean, no judgement, but I've never seen people like that, big and little in ways I don't get.

I THINK it's been long enough that I can confirm it. My lizard ate my tits. They're just gone, and he's grown even bigger, but I love him and he is such a good boy. What should I name him?

STRANGER STORIES

ANJA HENDRIKSE LIU (298 WORDS)

Honorable Mention

When she returns, she smells like a stranger. She's been out collecting, I know it immediately—though I'm not supposed to know. She wants to carry this burden, the weight of strangers' stories, alone.

It wasn't always this way. I remember one night, the only sleepover we had as girls. I'd promised to stay awake, but I nodded off. When I woke, mascara was running down her cheeks. She threw her arms around me. "Why didn't you stay awake? You promised."

"What? I'm sorry, I—"

She whispered, "At night, if no one's with me, I go out. People send me their stories. Everything they're worried about, everything that hurts them." Her fingers scratched at the rime of mascara. "I just wanted to stay here tonight."

We drifted apart after that.

Years later, we met again in a bar. She looked me up and down. "You've grown up!"

I couldn't tell this self-assured woman that I still woke in the night thinking of a ten-year-old broken promise. I couldn't ask if her whispered secret held true, if she was forced every night to collect emotions that people couldn't hold inside.

Instead, I gave her my number.

In the following nights, she hid her secret so well, I convinced myself I'd imagined it. Until tonight, when she returns, smelling like a stranger.

I think of the sleepover and how she clung to me, shaken by whatever she'd collected from that stranger.

I can't help myself. I open my eyes.

She's outlined in streetlight. I think she's crying; black makeup trails down her cheeks. Then the moonlight glints on one of the trails. It's darker than mascara, viscous.

Ink?

She feels me stir. She looks down.

With the ink of a stranger's stories dripping from her eye sockets, she smiles.

GUILTY PLEASURE READING

BRADLEY ROBERT PARKS (296 WORDS)

This was my eighth trip to the bathroom this morning. This time, though, I actually had to pee. But as soon as I unzipped, I had to fight the urge to re-read the script that crawled across my abdomen and down my hip.

"Did you get a new tat?" Walter. Of course he would look. Why couldn't they have put dividers between the urinals?

"Dude, no." I zipped up, casually as I could manage.

"C'mon. You have to let me see."

He wouldn't stop until I relented. "Watch the door." I pulled up my shirt and pushed my underwear down to show my hip. He leaned close, brow creasing as he read line after line of small, messy script, then stood abruptly.

"You have an Inkubus? You need an exorcist for that! I gotta cousin who's a priest."

"No!" I stuffed my shirtfront back into my slacks. "I want to see how this ends."

His eyes widened. "You like it. You're gonna end up like Ray."

"Don't be sick." Ray was a bum that panhandled in front of our build-ing, his skin so black with writing that he wept ink, sweated it, shirt collars stained black. "I'll stop when the story's finished."

On the /r/Inkubo *subreddit*, men transcribed the stories Inkubi left on their skin and shared experiences with their erotic nightly visitors.

Mine was not the best, but the story grabbed me. A hot young chef who could make a dish that satisfied the deepest desires of any man he slept with. The cooking scenes were so full of yearning, I wondered if the demon was a wannabe chef himself.

"Hey buddy, it's your career." Walter washed his hands and left.

I stayed in a stall, re-reading my left thigh for the ninth time today.

THE MUSE'S GIFT

FIONA MOORE (293 WORDS)

Honorable Mention

I met her at a women's bar, and I thought she said her name was "Kali." Her hair piled on her head, drinking wine spritzer. The dress code was denim and leather, so she should have looked out of place, not transcendent, in that Burning Man kaftan thing.

When we went back to my place, she drifted to my desk, ran her long onyx fingers over the notebooks, the contracts, the worn squares of the keyboard.

You write, she said. It was a statement, purred, triumphant.

I said something self-deprecating, like, mostly I stack supermarket shelves.

If you really want to succeed as a writer, she said, you have to bleed ink.

Yeah, I said. (I was kissing her fingers, working my way up.)

Do you want to bleed ink, Jen?

Sure. (I'd worked my way up and was working my way down.)

Then say it.

What?

Say it. Say you want to bleed ink.

Okay, I want to.

You have to say it all.

I want to bleed ink.

Say it!

I want to bleed ink!

YES!

Yes!

I bleed ink!
Bleed… ink…

∾

ABOUT TWO WEEKS later I went into the bathroom, pulled down my pants and there it was. Blue-black, glistening. Protean.

And every month after that, right at the same time. Blue-black, not red. Thick and viscous, smelling of indigo. Bringing forth a different kind of life, a different kind of children. The promise of new words.

The goddess Kali's supposed to be blue-black and shiny, too. But I'd misheard.

Her name was Cali.

Calliope.

Calliope, muse of writers. Maybe you get lucky, and you see her, or get even luckier and you fuck.

I don't stack shelves anymore, because I've learned.

Whom the muse loves, bleeds ink.

THE FINAL LINE

A.M. BURNS (294 WORDS)

Honorable Mention

Concentration didn't help stop the tired quivers in my hands. I had to finish. That was part of the spell. If the portrait wasn't completed in one sitting, it wouldn't work, and my years of training and questing for just the right ingredients would be for naught. How many times had I tried and failed? I'd lost count.

I dipped my quill in the luminescent ink. Even with all my preparations, I'd been a little surprised when the dragon's blood and manticore venom hadn't exploded when I combined them to make the precious, life-giving ink. The well-aged, enchanted, white stag's hide canvas glowed brighter and brighter with each line.

Would Mikial remember me? My beard had more than a little silver in it, while his would still be dark blond. I wasn't as strong as I had been when the dragon had killed him; at least I had been able to slay that dragon before my strength began to fail. If someone else had killed that great wyrm, my magic ink wouldn't be working.

The point of my phoenix quill raked across the bottom of the ceramic well.

I glanced at Mikial's face on the canvas. Only a few more lines.

Tilting the well. I managed to get a couple more drops out.

My hands shook harder as I connected the last line of Mikial's regal nose.

Years of spells washed over me, pushing me back.

Light burst from the canvas. I clinched my eyes tight.

A heavy musky scent struck me. Mikial's scent.

Strong fingers brushed my face.

"Rafi?" His voice was perfect.

"Mikial." I looked into a face I hadn't seen in a hundred years.

"You got old." He hugged me, and nothing else mattered. Every line was worth seeing him again.

FUTURE PERFECT
P.T. WYANT (299 WORDS)

She studied the teenage girl in the painting, the words "Self Portrait" in blood red across the top. "I wish," she murmured, gently tracing the figure's curves.

She propped a note against the painting, the ink blurred by teardrops.

"I know you think I'm gay. I'm not, and I can't go on living a lie. Yes, I like guys but I'm not one. This body is all wrong. This body isn't me. I'm a girl. I know you'll never accept me living as one, but I can die as one."

She'd made up her mind when she'd painted it; now all she had to do was follow through...

Now, while she was alone in the house.

She hoped she'd taken enough sleeping pills.

SHE STUMBLED INTO THE HALL. The door in the ceiling was closed, but the sound of footsteps overhead had awakened her, and she unfolded the steps.

Idiot. There could be an axe murderer up there. She nearly laughed; at least she wouldn't have to worry if she'd taken enough pills.

Boxes, old furniture, cobwebs. Nothing out of the ordinary except a reflection in the mirror of her great-grandmother's vanity. She looked behind her but she was alone. The reflection, an older version of her painting, smiled and nodded toward an envelope tucked into the mirror's frame, addressed to her. Not to her dead name, but to her chosen name, a name no one else knew.

"If you're reading this, it's not too late; you haven't killed us yet. I'm the future you, please give us – give yourself – a chance to live."

Inside was an article about a new art gallery, including a picture of the woman in the mirror standing next to the self-portrait in her room. Their eyes locked as she smiled and faded away.

RIGHT PLACE, RIGHT TIME
RYLEY BANKS (300 WORDS)

Honorable Mention

"Right place, right time" was inked in dark letters on the inside of my right thigh, inscribing my soulmate's first words to me. The phrase appeared as expected when I hit puberty on the first place they would touch my body. Everyone assumed, because the words weren't on my hands or arms like theirs, I didn't have a soulmate. And at thirty, I was beginning to think they were right.

"Daniel?" called a library volunteer. "Any luck?"

I'd been shelving when the volunteer had given me a book request, the patron waiting by the circulation desk. I'd seen him before, but never talked to him. Probably because he was absolutely *gorgeous*.

"Not yet." I sighed. No more shelves to search at ground-level.

"I'll check the night drop." The volunteer left me stranded.

No choice but to climb the terrifying rolling ladder to reach the highest bookshelves. My hands went clammy. But I couldn't look like a chicken in front of Hot Patron.

One rung, two, three, until I reached the top.

Refusing to look down, I scanned a row and—there. Shelved incorrectly.

Clinging to the ladder, I stretched, fingers brushing the spine—

The ladder rolled.

I paused, midair, and plummeted past the shelves, bracing for the shattering impact.

A hand gripped my thigh, halting my descent. An arm wrapped around my waist and I grabbed on. We tumbled to the floor.

"You saved my life." I turned over to thank—whoa. Hot Patron was breathtaking up close, all strong jaw and lush lips. One look and it was clear —my heart had known him forever.

Eyes wide, he lifted the arm I'd touched, what I'd just said inked there.

"Right place, right time," he whispered.

Laughing, I stroked my inner thigh. His hand covered mine.

His book could wait.

ALL MYTHS ARE TRUE (BUT SOME ARE TRUER THAN OTHERS)
RORY NI COILEAIN (293 WORDS)

The priestesses of Nakeshta, She-Who-Writes, claim that the world was created when their goddess first wrote the inner Name of each being into Her book of life. The priestesses of Navyanta, She-Who-Shapes, hold that each unique being is their goddess' thumbprint in the wet clay of the world she made, Her sign and seal.

NAKESHTA SANK into the steaming water, sighing blissfully. "Do you know how long it's been since I've had a night without a deadline?"

"Aeons," her wife replied. "Me too. Why Mother decided she needed 200 new worlds ready to launch by Heirsday next, I can't fathom."

In addition to calming Nakeshta's frazzled nerves, the steam was making Navyanta's mahogany hair kink in ways that reminded Nakeshta how *very* long it had been since she'd been able to toy with it.

As if reading Nakeshta's mind, Navyanta reached out with a foot, teasing her toes under the water.

"Champagne?" Candlelight danced in Navyanta's deep brown eyes.

"Do I dare?"

"Oh, come on. The kid's sound asleep. Even if she wakes up, Lish will find us."

Nakeshta hesitated. And in that hesitation, both goddesses heard a bump. One that sounded exactly like a pixie wrapped in a bedsheet colliding with a doorframe.

"Workroom," the bedsheet croaked as the mothers levitated out of the hot tub.

Workroom, indeed. Living ink puddled on Nakeshta's worktable, the floor, previously blank sheets of vellum. A red-haired toddler held aloft a sphere of still-soft porcelain, perfect until ink-smeared hands had left finger-marks all over it.

"Remind me whose good idea it was to name this child She-Who-Meddles?" Navyanta sounded as if she was trying not to cry. Or laugh.

"Mother's. Are you going to fire that one?"

"No choice. Deadline."

"Pretty!" Nasuumta crowed.

"Pretty. Bedtime."

RISOTTO NERO

C.L. MCCARTNEY (300 WORDS)

Honorable Mention

"This recipe, *giovanotto*, is my family's greatest treasure."

Signor Polani smiled with secret satisfaction.

"Playwrights, *poeti*—they march across Europe just for a mouthful. And today, Oscar Wilde will taste pure *inspiration*."

Tomaso the kitchen boy did not care for famed English writers. Instead, he daydreamed of a certain singing gondolier; a handsome, golden-voiced tenor, who passed the restaurant each day.

"Take fresh pages and wild garlic," Polani lectured. "Slice the words thin and braise them in their own ink. *Lightly*, lest the ideas grow tough…"

Tomaso had composed a poem for his gondolier, pouring out his heart. Now the stanzas sat folded in his pocket.

Soon, the gondolier's voice would echo across the Rialto, Tomaso would rush outside and—

"My ink!" *Giovanotto*, where is my ink?!"

Tomaso looked up. Ash-faced, Polani jabbed his finger at an empty jug.

Ice lanced Tomaso's chest. "I went first thing, signor!"

He'd bought the complete works of Sappho, leatherbound. After dutifully despining and slicing the pages, he'd pressed them into a pint of fresh, black ink.

All gone…

Polani sank to the floor, moaning. "No taste of inspiration. *Mio Dio!* The novel he'll never write…"

Whilst his master sobbed, Tomaso fingered the poem in his pocket—a terrible idea forming. Could he do it? After battling for days to transmute his love into words. *Could* he?

Slowly, Tomaso drew out the poem.

"Signor..."

A delighted gasp—then the page was snatched away.

Polani stirred and simmered, chopped, and pressed. Straining, he reclaimed a single measure of ink from Tomaso's page and stirred it through the dish. Finally, he set the steaming bowl upon the counter: Perfect rice grains, coated in unctuous black, glistening with desire and love.

"Quickly, *giovanotto!* For Signor Wilde!"

Tomaso stared, forlorn, as a distant tenor voice began to sing.

JUST A NUDGE

E. W. MURKS (299 WORDS)

"Hello?"

Certainly, he was lost. Only three people had wandered into the shop all week.

"I'm sorry. We're closed." I finished my inventory and stood up. My head hit the counter with a thud.

"Ow!"

He offered his hand, and I took it.

"Are you alright, Mr. Peligree?" he asked.

He knew my name and seemed familiar, somehow. Perhaps a former pupil. He stood there, all freckles with a dimpled chin, his thick red mane pulled to one side. Eyes a piercing blue.

"Yes. Thank you." He was still holding my hand. He looked at me sheepishly and let go.

"Are you open tomorrow?"

"Yes, but I can't turn you away now, can I?" I smiled. "What are you looking for?"

"Well, I was wondering, do you have any... binding ink?" he asked.

I stepped back. Binding inks were forbidden. Reading the right words penned in the right ink, was roughly the equivalent of a love potion.

"I'm sorry. We're not that kind of shop."

"But I heard-"

"You heard wrong."

"Maybe something weaker? Just... a nudge?" His hand was on top of mine. It was warm. Very warm.

I sighed and pulled a small bottle of ink from below the counter. I held it up to the light. Specks of silver swam in a sea of rich purple. I handed it to him.

"How much?" he asked.

"It's yours."

He smiled and thanked me profusely. As I watched him go, he turned and waved. I waved back, standing at the window until he was gone.

A few days later, I discovered an envelope under the shop door. I broke the seal and retrieved the note inside.

I began to read but then quickly folded it up. "Foolish boy," I said, shaking my head.

Because I needed no nudge.

THE INKER, THE CAT AND THE PARROT

BARBARA KRASNOFF (296 WORDS)

Honorable Mention

Ginger had wanted to talk to the new girl for two weeks now. Her name was Lisa, and she had shiny black hair that hung to her shoulders, large dark eyes, and thin, elegant fingers. Every time Ginger glanced at her, she had trouble breathing. She was totally, incurably, in love.

The Inkers, as they were known, were 100 young women who sat in a large room, carefully tracing the lines of animated animals on cels with thin strokes of black ink. It was hard, careful work, but this was 1938, the Depression was still on, and the job at the animation studio paid well.

Ginger was a good inker, but she had ruined two cels because she couldn't stop herself from wondering about Lisa, who sat three desks away. Did she have a chance? What if Lisa had a boyfriend? Or, worse, a girlfriend?

She bent close to the cel she was inking, which portrayed a cartoon cat staring at a caged parrot. A tear dropped on the surface. "Watch it!" the cat said irritably. "You've nearly ruined my ear!"

"She's obsessing about that girl," said the parrot. "We'd better do something about it."

Ginger stared, dumbfounded, at the cel. The cat turned its head and looked directly at her. "She's working on a scene in which I'm jumping at the parrot. Do you want me to ask if she's free for dinner?"

"Um—okay," Ginger said. She bit her lip. Was she crazy? Had she spent too many hours staring at the cells, inking the lines that surrounded the cartoon characters?

"It's all set," said the parrot. "Tonight, after work."

Ginger raised her head and looked over at Lisa, who met her eyes and smiled.

"Now please be more careful!" demanded the cat.

SO LET IT BE WRITTEN, SO LET IT BE DONE

S R JONES (299 WORDS)

"We cannot just stand by."

Amoten stared at body on the slab in front of him. It was blank now, wrapped as it was in layers of clean white linen. He knew what Sanum was saying, of course, but he was a priest of the tombs, and his duties had nothing to do with the events that had led to this. The only laws he cared for were the ones the Gods laid out for him: make the bodies clean, make them dry, and bind them in the spells that would see them reborn in the Afterlife. It wasn't his place to care about who they'd been or what they'd done, and yet, he felt a weight on his shoulders that he couldn't explain.

"What can we do now, Sanum? Death cannot be undone,"

"We can do what is *right*,"

"There *is* no right here. There is only what *is*, and the murder is done. Nobody helped her."

"But *we* can," said Sanum. "A few drops of ink, my friend. Just a few changed words, and there can be some justice here- not in this life, but in the next." He glanced at the shadows, anxious of spies, perhaps, and lowered his voice. "Please, do not let them bury her as a man. Is she to suffer in the next life as much as they made her suffer in this one?"

Amoten sighed deeply. It would be easier to do nothing, but the Gods had charged him with taking care of the dead. Inaction did not feel like caring; action, however, was surely heresy.

"No. We will not scribble over sacred prayers," he said at last, his mind made up. "We must re-do them completely. Bring me my pens, Sanum, and we shall write her soul into Paradise."

RENAMING
ZIGGY SCHUTZ (299 WORDS)

JUDGE'S CHOICE - E.M. Hamill

Honor's skin is an oil spill of bad decisions.

Wrong choices immortalized by ink-dipped fingers, hauntings of kind touches now just stains.

They are a living graveyard. Both the haunting and the haunted.

And when they pass through a town, never daring to linger, not wanting to infect others with this creeping darkness, people avert their eyes, fear heavy on their tongues.

Honor does not blame them. If they had anyone to call their own, they would do the same thing. Had done the same thing, a lifetime ago. Threw themself on a curse, to save a place they'd once called home.

But monsters don't have homes.

Or names to be greeted by.

They continue on.

THEY ARE BEING FOLLOWED.

This happens, sometimes. Someone with visions of being some kind of hero, saving the world from a creature who is only trying to survive.

These heroes' swords cut deep, and darkness spills out of every wound, drowning them while Honor watches.

Maybe it's not fair, that they should destroy these brave, foolish warriors so easily.

But Honor had also been brave and foolish once, and they had not been spared.

And for all of their inkblot existence, they do not wish to die.

And so these heroes drown.

THIS HERO HAS NO SWORD, just a cane that has seen better days, shaved head showing off a troubadour's tattoos.

He smiles, and it cuts as much as any blade. Kindness always does.

"Come to kill me?" Honor asks, and he laughs, shakes out his skirts and sits next to her.

"Do you know the difference between a hero and a monster?"

"No."

"A good story," he says, and dips his quill in their darkness, starts to write.

Stories can infect, too.

IN THE NEXT TOWN, they all know Honor's name.

This story had my attention from the first sentence, all the way to the end. The final line instills a sense of hope . Knowledge dispels fear. It's the only one I read out loud to someone else because I had to share some of the imagery. Well done!

—E.M. Hamill

PROOF IN THE TELLING

RINA YOUNGBLOOD (300 WORDS)

Honorable Mention

I am sharpening a needle when it begins to sing noiselessly in my hand. In the vibration of the bone is the cry of a seer hawk from which it had come. Mother Tahra felled it last spring, even as its talons savaged her thigh; Mother Aissa did the butchering.

"We have a guest," I say, and the needle trembles with anticipation.

Mother Tahra reaches for her cane and begins to rise, but Mother Aissa rests an ink-stained hand on her shoulder. "I'll get the door," she says, and I wonder if I will ever share the coal-burn warmth of the look my mothers share.

The visitor's eyes are rimmed red. Only a few years older than myself—old enough to be conscripted into the border wars, but as he proffers his coin, I see the missing fingers that bar him from bearing a sword in the king's name.

There is silence as he is seated. His question need not be spoken in order for us to give him the answer. Tahra takes my sharpened needle. Aissa mixes the inks: ash from the hawk, blood from her own veins.

Today it is Tahra who carves the prophecy across the supplicant's palm. An hour's labour before she wipes the needle and Aissa leans forward to frown at the raw shape. She beckons to me. "Read."

The tattoo stings the eye to look upon, like sunlight cutting across unsettled waters, but the fortune is clear.

"No," I read, "your husband will not live."

The youth does not weep, in that moment.

But when he leaves the cottage, I watch through the window to see him fall to his knees. His hunched shoulders tremble.

"Come away," Tahra says behind me. "We may read his fortune, but it is not ours to share."

ABOUT QUEER SCI FI & OTHER WORLDS INK

Queer Sci Fi: We started QSF in 2014 as a place for writers and readers of LGBTQ+ spec fic—sci fi, fantasy, paranormal, horror and the like—to talk about their favorite books, share writing tips, and increase queer representation in romance and mainstream genre markets. Helmed by admins Scott, Angel, Ben and Ryane, QSF includes a blog, a vibrant FB discussion group, a twitter page, and an annual flash fiction contest that resulted in this book you are now reading.

Website: http://www.queerscifi.com
FB Discussion Group: facebook.com/groups/qsfdiscussions/
MeWe Discussion Group: https://mewe.com/
group/5c6c8bf7aef4005aa6bf3e12
Promo/News Page: facebook.com/queerscifi/
Twitter: Twitter.com/queerscifi/

Also by Queer Sci Fi:

Discovery (2016 - out of print)
Flight (2017 - out of print)
Renewal (2017 - out of print Sept 2020)
Impact (2018 - Other Worlds Ink)
Migration (2019 - Other Worlds Ink)

Other Worlds Ink: The brainchild of J. Scott Coatsworth and his husband, Mark Guzman. OWI publishes Scott's works and the annual Queer Sci Fi flash fiction series. We also create blog tours for authors, do eBook formatting and graphics work, and offer Wordpress site support for authors.